Try AS I SMITE

BRIMSTONE  INC.

Try AS I SMITE

BRIMSTONE ✪ INC.

ABIGAIL OWEN

Entangled Publishing, LLC
10940 S Parker Rd
Suite 327
Parker, CO 80134
rights@entangledpublishing.com

Amara is an imprint of Entangled Publishing, LLC.

Edited by Heather Howland
Cover design by Bree Archer
Cover photography by IgorVetushko/Deposit Photos
Voysla and peeterv/Getty Images

Manufactured in the United States of America

First Edition October 2020

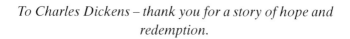

To Charles Dickens – thank you for a story of hope and redemption.

Chapter One

News of a mage going mad and lashing out with magic would typically raise alarms, but today, yet another such report in his hands was the least of Alasdair Blakesley's worries.

A bigger problem had just walked into his office.

His long-time personal assistant, Agnes. She entered laden with a tray. Presumably his lunch.

"Thai today," she sang out.

He had no idea what alerted him that something was seriously wrong. The tone of her voice probably. Serious, semi-snappy Agnes did *not* use a singsongy voice. Ever.

Nearing her late sixties—though she refused to retire, informing him that he'd be a pathetic mess without her, which was true—Agnes wore her steel-gray hair severely scraped back from her face, never a strand out of place. Like her hair, she was scarily efficient at her job, and as abrasive as a Brillo pad when she deemed it necessary.

A voice like a sweet little mouse was not in her repertoire.

In fact, having to order him lunch because, as often happened, he'd let his job distract him from the time, would irritate her. As the head of the Covens Syndicate—the body of witches and warlocks who monitored, policed, protected, and ruled the established covens of magi throughout the world— he found his focus on the needs of his people overruled eating. Brillo voice would be more likely right now.

He watched her closely as she set the tray down on the round table in the corner. Made of petrified wood, the table stood out like a sore thumb from the rest of his ultra-modern office, which was all glass, black leather, and chrome. With a cheerfulness also nothing like his Agnes, she arranged the plates to her liking, then glanced up.

And blinked. Because Alasdair had taken her distraction as an opportunity to move to the door, which he shut with a quiet *snick*.

"Can I get you anything else, sir?"

Sir? Alasdair reached for his power, allowing the magic to flow through like electric current over a wire, his fingertips buzzing with it.

"Yes," he said in a quiet voice any friend, and most enemies, would recognize meant he was holding back rage. "You can tell me what you've done with Agnes."

The imposter tipped her head to the side, doing a fantastic imitation of a confused frown. "I don't understand, sir. Of course it's me—"

With a single thought, a slithering line of electricity shot from his fingers, aimed at the fake in front of him.

She dropped all pretense of misunderstanding, and, with a snarl that raised the hairs on the back of his neck, jumped out of the way, only to land lightly on her feet, straightening from his assistant's customary slightly hunched posture, eyes and mouth turned the color of gangrene, the color leaching into the surrounding skin, as though evidence of an infection of the soul.

At least Alasdair knew what he was dealing with.

Demon.

Which meant he couldn't kill it. He'd learned that the hard way a long time ago. Demons possessed human bodies, their corporeal forms too noticeable in the human realm to be used. If he killed the demon, he killed the vessel, and he couldn't do that to Agnes. Which meant he'd need to bind it.

Please let this be a lower level demon.

Alasdair raised his hands in the air, calling on his magic. Immediately, a violent wind slashed through the office and tore at his immaculate suit jacket. The demon didn't even sway with the impact. A glass statue in one corner wobbled and fell with a crash, shattering into a million shards, which Alasdair immediately summoned, using his magic to hurl at the demon.

With a swipe of its arm, the thing inside Agnes diverted the shards around its body. They embedded in the wall, sounding like a thousand tiny bullets hitting their mark with sharp, popping thuds.

"You'll have to do better than that," the demon sneered, its deep, scratchy voice at odds with Agnes's body.

It lunged, streaking with inhuman speed across the room at him. The winds he'd summoned had reached hurricane force but might not as well have been blowing for all the detriment they posed. Alasdair held still, waiting for the right movement to strike. Waiting for its sickly sweet breath to hit his face before he struck.

The words of his spell punched through his mind, and, in an instant, a length of cord materialized in his hands, glowing bright white with energy. At his will, it shot forward to wrap around the demon charging him.

The thing was fast, and damn strong, and Alasdair didn't time it exactly right, the cord missing one of the thing's arms. Not that it mattered. The creature screamed with agony as the holy bondage that Alasdair had summoned from his childhood home where it had been hidden for ages set the demon's skin sizzling everywhere the rope touched.

Still, the demon wasn't going down without a fight. Agnes's neatly manicured nails turned to onyx claws, and it slashed at him, even as it fell to the ground, held secure by his bonds.

Alasdair wasn't quite fast enough to get out of its way. Jagged pain burned through his skin as dark red patches bloomed slick and wet against the pristine white of his button-down shirt.

He disregarded the wounds, following the demon to the ground. The rope was ancient and would hold it for only so long.

Bringing all his weight to bear, he knelt on the demon's free arm and placed a hand to its forehead, positioned to avoid now-razor-sharp, snapping teeth. Closing his eyes, Alasdair whispered the words that would bind the demon physically as well as making sure it didn't escape to another body.

Agnes would hate being trapped inside her own hell, her magic trapped with her, and he didn't blame her for that. But until Alasdair could summon one of the mages who specialized in demon extraction, he had no choice.

With the last uttered incantation, the possessed creature went still and quiet, arms and legs straight out, face frozen in a grotesque grimace, as though petrified. Slowly, Alasdair rose to his feet. Keeping careful watch on the thing, he moved behind his desk and picked up the phone.

"Help me."

Every muscle in his body tensed to the point of cramping at the sound of Agnes's true voice. The black void of her eyes turned brown and human again. "Help me," she croaked.

Mother goddess.

Anyone with a heart would be tempted to go to her, but what he knew of demons held him still.

"He's going to kill me." She sounded so desperate, helpless.

The tension in him eased a fraction. Nope. Not Agnes. She would know better, and she would *never* beg. The real her would be swearing a blue streak about now, and probably even shock the doomed soul inhabiting her body.

Ignoring the creature, he dialed the number that would get him what he needed. Within moments, a team of witches and warlocks trained for battle, trained to protect, invaded his office. As soon as he knew they had Agnes and her current parasitic invader in hand, Alasdair snatched his phone from a drawer and strode from the room.

Suddenly all the reports of inexplicable crazed bouts among his people made sense. They weren't crazed...they were fucking possessed.

If anyone had a reason to fear demon possession, he did. But the world, most of whom didn't know magic truly did exist, would come to live in terror of them if they took over enough mages.

"Don't leave me with him inside me!" Agnes screamed, her pleading voice following him out of the room.

Leashing a flinch, he stopped at the elevator where the leader of the team, Micah Aluron, joined him, sharp eye taking in the scene with unsmiling purpose. "Orders, sir?"

"Hold that thing until I get back. Gag her if you have to."

"Get back?" Micah asked. "Aren't you supposed to be having dinner with your sister tonight?"

Dammit, he'd forgotten all about Hestia and Christmas Eve. "I can't. This needs to be addressed immediately."

Micah gave a quick nod. "Where are you going?"

Had this been anyone other than his old friend, Alasdair wouldn't have bothered to answer. Only, this was Micah, a man who'd saved his ass on at least three different occasions. The time in Barcelona didn't count, of course. Alasdair had returned the favor even more times than that. A situation that meant they trusted each other. Implicitly.

"We have a demon problem," he said, and couldn't control the fury that turned his voice dark. "This isn't a singular incident. It's one of many."

"Shit." Even Micah turned ashy at that. "You think all the other reports are possessions?"

Alastair nodded.

Micah seemed to be of the same mind. "It takes a hell of a lot of magic to exorcise a single demon."

And they were looking at more than one. A horde maybe, hopefully not a legion. Alasdair's own power didn't stretch that far, and even the entire Syndicate working together might not be enough. He refused to kill those afflicted unless he had to.

"Magic may not be able to fix this, but I know a…person who might be able to help."

The enigmatic woman who'd been a burr under his metaphorical saddle since he met her. He would *much* rather have gone begging for a place in her bed to exorcise the spell she'd cast that seemed to grip him harder with every encounter they had.

Having to grovel for help, on the other hand, was the last thing he'd pictured himself ever having to do.

He should have known better.

• • •

"I need to see Delilah."

In her private office, windows overlooking the Denver downtown with the snow-covered Rocky Mountains hazy in the late morning light, Delilah raised her head.

No mistaking those deep tones, even over the Christmas music piping softly through the office. Hell, she'd fantasized about that smooth-as-sin voice as she'd pleasured herself at night. Every night for over a year. An anomaly for her.

Alasdair Blakesley.

The control-obsessed leader of the Covens Syndicate who had a chip on his shoulder the size of a large building when it came to his magic-only policies, which meant he didn't appreciate her taking on clients that impacted his kind in any way.

Well, too damn bad.

Stubborn, conceited, and unbearably sarcastic, Alasdair was a man who preferred to have the upper hand in every situation. It had taken her about two and three-quarter seconds to figure that much out. By some miracle, she'd managed to avoid crossing his path until last year when, unbeknownst to him, she'd helped his lead witch-hunter find love in an unconventional way.

Most of her ways were unconventional.

Since then, Alasdair had popped up in her life, her office, and even tried to summon her to his location, almost once a month, if not more. All on the pretext of "checking in" to see if she'd picked up any more cases related to magic wielders.

Unfortunately, to her everlasting resentment, her body turned to molten fire every damn time he came near. In fact, the sensation was already thrumming through her blood at the sound of him in her outer office, setting her teeth on edge. Her grudging respect for him—which she would never disclose, his ego didn't need the boost—only made it worse.

What in the world was he doing in her office? On Christmas Eve, no less. She might avoid the holiday like the plague, but she knew mages celebrated.

Curiosity had her out of her seat and halfway to the open doorway when the voices grew louder.

"You can't go in there, sir." Her personal assistant and bodyguard, Naiobe, was as near to shouting as the freed djinn got.

Delilah sped up before Naiobe could get into a magical power struggle with one of the most formidable mages on the planet. Mentally burying what she refused to label as tumbling excitement at seeing him, she paused in the doorway. The man towering over her assistant, who glared back, nose twitching but undaunted, didn't seem to notice.

Delilah crossed her arms, leaning against the doorjamb, and pasted a deliberately provocative smile to her lips. "If the next words out of your mouth are, 'Don't you know who I am?', I'm going to be very disappointed in you, Alasdair."

He rearranged his posture in a hurry, straightening sharply, shoulders back. He even plucked at the cuffs of his immaculate three-piece suit as though he hadn't just been losing his shit. "Delilah," he greeted coolly.

What? No smart comeback?

He really wears that suit.

She swept the thought into a corner of her mind littered with similar thoughts about this man.

She tipped her chin up. "To what do I owe the dubious honor? You realize tomorrow is Christmas, right?"

He didn't respond as he swung away from Naiobe with a countenance gone hard as marble. Unless she missed her guess, the warlock was in a thundering rage that had nothing to do with being barred admission to her. Which meant this wasn't his usual "spy on Delilah" drop-by. Interesting.

"May we speak in private?" he demanded more than asked.

Naiobe sent his back a baleful glare.

"Of course." Delilah waved him inside, projecting more calm than the riot of conflicting emotions and anticipation currently churning in her belly. She paused long enough to send Naiobe an inquiring look.

"He's in a mood," she was informed through gritted

teeth.

Wow. Alasdair had really managed to get under her usually unflappable assistant's skin. "I noticed. Maybe you should bring some popcorn. This could be quite a showdown."

That got Naiobe to ease up with a chuckle. Delilah winked and followed the man into her office, closing the door behind her with a click. She could handle Alasdair Blakesley.

He stood with his back to her, staring out the wall of windows that faced the mountains to the west of Denver. "Popcorn? Really?"

Wow. He must be off his game if that's all he had.

She walked on bare feet across the plush carpet to her desk. She'd gotten up with such haste, she'd forgotten her damn shoes.

He turned, clearly about to speak, then, in slow motion his gaze dropped to her unshod feet and remained there. Was that a twitch at the corner of his mouth?

Double damn. She hated being wrong-footed. Literally. Delilah ignored him as she went to her desk and snatched the black Louis Vuiton stilettos from underneath.

"Can I get you water?" she asked as she came back around, waving at a more comfortable space nearer the floor-to-ceiling windows that included a rustic-looking leather couch she'd spent more than one night sleeping on and matching leather chairs.

"No, thank you." He hesitated, seeming to have to prepare himself. "I need your help."

Delilah paused with her ass halfway to the couch. He did not just say that. *The* Alasdair Blakesley, who despised her involvement in anything magic related, had not just said those words.

She straightened. "You need my help?" she repeated, deadpan.

"Yes."

"*You* need *my* help," she said again, just to be certain.

"Let's not make a big deal of it."

Like she'd pass up this opportunity. "Naiobe," she raised her voice and called out. "Definitely bring the popcorn. You're never going to believe this…"

He crossed his arms with a baleful glare. "Hilarious. I've never laughed so hard."

"Really?" She blinked, all wide-eyed innocence. "That's a surprise. I didn't think you knew how to laugh."

He clamped his lips shut.

Score one for her. Because there was no way she believed this request was real. This had to be a test, or his version of some gods-awful joke. But she'd play along for a minute. This night was her most despised of the year, so even a round or two with Alasdair was a welcome distraction.

Seating herself without waiting for him, when he didn't bother to join her, she slipped her shoes onto her feet, smoothed her cream-colored skirt over her thighs, then crossed her ankles and settled her hands primly in her lap, fingers laced in a subtle steepling.

Based on the way his gaze flicked to the movement followed by a tightening of his lips, he got the message. She was in charge here.

"So…you need my help?" She couldn't help saying it one more time.

"I knew this was a bad idea," he muttered.

"It wasn't mine."

"Gods above, will you please *listen*?" Alasdair snapped.

Whoa. Delilah stilled, taking a closer look.

On the outside he appeared his usual impeccable self. Conservative black custom suit tailored to perfection to his broad shoulders, trim hips, and powerful legs. Jet black hair cropped short, though slightly longer on top, swept to the side, not a follicle out of place. Cleanly shaven jaw which, already sharply angled, appeared closer to the set of granite today.

A tell. She doubted many ever got to see the man this riled.

When she sat quietly and waited, Alasdair's eyes narrowed as though he didn't quite trust her. In a casual move at odds with the tension riding his body, he slipped his hands into his pockets and stared at her with bright blue eyes.

Delilah mentally sorted through a list of her recent clients in her head, along with a quick rehash of her last few encounters with this man. What in heaven's name had brought him to her in such a state?

Granted, kicking him out of the dance club in Miami where she'd been helping a particularly troubled mermaid, she might've gone a teensy bit overboard making her point. No doubt he hadn't appreciated finding himself teleported to Siberia.

That had been over a week ago.

Thank the powers that Alasdair didn't know why she'd done that. He'd touched her arm. A casual move, only her body had lit up like fireworks at the New Year. From that one tiny, ridiculous contact. Sending him away had been an act of sheer desperation.

The most frustrating part was, she couldn't See him. See his future or how it impacted hers. See where this troubling *wanting* when it came to him was going to end. Her most secret and precious gift, her ability as a Seer, allowed her to help her clients in ways no one else ever could.

But Alasdair Blakely was a blank. A black hole of nothing. That never happened except around vampires and ghosts, because, technically, they were dead. He wasn't one of those.

Meanwhile, he stood statue-still, continuing to stare at her.

Delilah sighed. "Alasdair. I can't do anything if you don't

tell me why you've come—"

"I have a demon problem." He practically bit off each word.

Every ounce of levity left her body in a *whoosh*. She tried not to show by even a whisper of a twitch how that statement hit her. *No, no, no. Not demons.*

"What kind of demon problem?" she asked slowly, proud that her voice didn't give away the sudden tightening in her chest, as though a yeti's pet elephant sat on top of her, cutting off her air.

"Multiple reports, twenty in the last week, of rage and unleashed magic resulting in injuries," he said. "No deaths so far, but it's only a matter of time."

Interesting. "How do you know for sure what you're dealing with?" *Please don't be demons. Anything but those.* "It could be any number of—"

"My assistant, Agnes, has been possessed. Definitely demon. I've…had a run-in with a demon before."

Well…fuck.

Alasdair slid into the chair opposite her. Even projecting his usual imperturbable disposition, tension was coming off him in tangible waves. She was surprised the man wasn't vibrating with it or manifesting magic to bleed it off. Not that she'd blame him.

Demons. It *would* have to be those, wouldn't it?

Delilah resisted the urge to uncross and recross her legs under the intentness of his gaze. "I'm sorry, but I don't deal with demons. Hard rule."

His thick brows snapped down over his eyes in an impressive scowl. "You don't deal—" He bit off the words. "What you mean is you don't help witches."

She pressed her lips together over defensive words that wanted to tumble out, limiting herself to a narrowing of her eyes. Ever off-balance around him in the most frustrating ways. Anyone else, and she wouldn't give two figs for ruffling feathers. She'd never experienced any desire to explain her actions or defend herself before. Why now? And why to him? "You know that's not true, or I wouldn't have helped Rowan Masters."

The red-haired witch, now married to Greyson Masters, Alasdair's lead witch-hunter enforcing the Syndicate's laws. Rowan was as powerful as they came. Excepting, perhaps, the man sitting in front of her right now. However, that previous situation had had nothing to do with demons. Or... not directly at least.

Alasdair's lip curled. Hell, even the man's sneer was controlled. But then he gave his head a shake, and a glimpse of vulnerability took her righteous anger away in an instant. "You're right..."

Not exactly an apology, but more than he'd given her in the past.

He shot to his feet. "So why won't you take me...us...on as a client?"

Interesting slip, and the gods knew she wished she could help them. Maybe a little spell wouldn't hurt. One to locate—

The second even a whisper of a thought of getting involved surfaced, a tightening sensation, as though metal cuffs around her wrists were clamping down hard, told her she was treading on dangerous ground. If she took it further, her skin would start to visibly chafe and then blister. Good thing her long-sleeved blouse of green chiffon covered the spots.

The same magic that shackled her wouldn't allow her to speak of it, either, so she couldn't even explain.

"I just..." She allowed herself the small act of blowing out a long breath. "I can't."

"Fuck." The quietly spat word, even as he held perfectly still saying it, sent a flinch through her.

His desperation was tangible, thick in the air. She regretted teasing him earlier now, because demons were as serious as it got.

"I may know someone else who can help." Though... because that person *could* help, didn't mean she would. The tightness cinched harder around Delilah's wrists, and she had to school her features not to show the pain, nearly glancing down to see if the skin around her wrists was turning red yet.

"Someone who can help?" He repeated her words in a tone that said he still couldn't believe she was turning him down.

Sorry, she mentally apologized. *Anything else, and I would have stepped in.*

Delilah offered him a shrug, for once not meaning to antagonize him, though the way his brows snapped together, she had. She rose to her feet to cross the room. Bringing up her computer, she pretended to hunt for information she already had memorized. Then wrote down an address on a slip of paper.

She straightened to find he'd moved on silent feet to stand across the desk from her. Resisting the need to take a step back, away from all that enticing, leashed energy, she held it out to him. "You'll find this...woman...is an expert on what you're dealing with. She may be of assistance."

He didn't take it. Just stared at her hard, accusation in the darkening blue of his eyes, turning them almost navy. If she didn't know him better, she'd say he was taking this personally. As though she'd wronged him somehow.

"I'm sorry I can't do more." Delilah bit the inside of her cheek. Dammit. Rule #1 in her business was no demons. Rule #2 was never apologize. Besides, she was trying here, dammit.

He shook his head, expression confounded. "I expected more from you," he said softly.

She swallowed.

"My people are in danger. You, the woman who helps everyone with a seemingly unending list of issues, won't help?" A bitter sort of disappointment filled his eyes, a direct hit to her heart, which usually she did a better job protecting.

Delilah locked her lips against another apology and shook the paper. "A smart man would take this."

A cauldron of emotion swirled and bubbled in his eyes. The disappointment definitely hit hardest. With another shake of his head, he snatched the paper from her hand and stalked to the door.

"I'll be sure to pass on this experience to anyone interested in your future services," he tossed over his shoulder. Then he was gone, leaving the door open between her office and Naiobe's.

As soon as the telltale *thunk* of the outer door closing reached her, Delilah waved a hand and her own door slammed shut so hard papers on her desk fluttered to the ground. She sank into her chair and held up her wrists. Sure enough, angry red welts appeared where the magical shackles bound her.

"Fuck," she breathed.

Because she would have done a hell of a lot more than hand him an address. If she could.

With a shaking hand, she picked up her cell phone and dialed. A sultry voice on the other end answered. "Hello?"

"Mom? A man will be coming to visit you any second. Please do what you can for him."

Chapter Two

Alasdair prided himself on his ability to read a person, but Delilah—and he still didn't know her last name—baffled the fuck out of him.

He didn't like it.

Especially when he'd allowed himself to fantasize about wrapping his fist in that long, dark hair and plumbing those lush lips with demanding kisses as he thrust into her sweet body. She smelled of cherry blossoms. He'd finally pinpointed the subtle floral note in her office the first time he'd "dropped by" for a surprise visit.

That time—which had involved her calling him a control freak and him calling her a rabble-rouser—had gone way better than this one. The woman could make a glacier lose its cool.

And yet his mind insisted on overriding his common sense and providing fantasies of a time and place where they were on the same side.

A weakness, he could see now.

He'd seen the types of clients she handled. Her

involvement with Rowan and Greyson had given him the impression Delilah had a guardian angel complex. Someone who liked to use whatever gifts she had in her possession to help the underdogs and lost causes.

After that incident, he'd investigated her. Money and power didn't seem to be a motivation beyond building her business. No one seemed to know what powers Delilah possessed herself, but she had an impressive network of contractors and supernaturally gifted people who owed her favors. Likely even more impressive than what he'd been able to unearth.

She used that network to fix supernatural problems for paranormal creatures of all types, creeds, and spectrums. Anything from matchmaking, to job placement, to healings, to personal investigations, to relocations and creating alternate identities, and more. There didn't seem to be any problem she couldn't handle. Except, apparently, mass exorcisms.

Why? Because she couldn't stand *him*? Was she that petty?

Alasdair wouldn't have thought so. Perhaps he'd allowed a slowly growing regard for what she did combine with a festering need to claim her luscious body blind him to who she was as a person. He'd thought, beneath all that defiance, that she had a heart and a conscience.

Clearly he'd got that wrong.

The thought soured in his head, like even thinking the words introduced poison into his thoughts. But damned if he should be giving her any leeway here. He'd been prepared to pay, as much as it took. Prepared to grovel even. Not having answers himself stuck in his craw. While he prided himself on refusing to give in to the illusion of being all powerful, it still rankled. Magic, even for one as formidable as he, wasn't going to fix a demon problem when the multitude he suspected were coming were involved.

Hold them off, at best.

Channeling his frustration with Delilah and the entire situation, Alasdair pulled it into the whispered spell that teleported him directly outside a home in…he glanced around his surroundings with a frown. In the middle of New York City? Upper West Side if he wasn't mistaken. His gaze skated up the front of the white limestone-sided house with impressive relief work carved into the facade. Five stories. *Not* an apartment.

The doorbell was answered by the epitome of a stiff butler who left him standing in the foyer, which might be the most marbled room Alasdair had ever encountered. The floors, stairs, and even walls were decorated in a white swirling marble with a star pattern in black and gold on the floor and small onyx squares spreading out from there.

He'd been born to wealth and privilege, used to the upper echelons of wiccan society, even after his parents' deaths, but this was a bit much. The only things not marble in the space were the shiny black iron balustrades of an epic curving staircase and the matching scrolling iron grills over each of the downstairs windows and the front door.

Not a single Christmas decoration in sight. Not that all beings celebrated, but it was a small clue into who or what Delilah had sent him to. Meanwhile, magical energy pulsed from those grills, skating across his skin, almost undetectable. Wards?

Who the hell *had* Delilah sent him to?

"Mr. Blakesley?" He turned from his impatient perusal of the room to find a woman descending the curving staircase. Possibly the most beautiful woman he'd ever seen in real life, other than Delilah who, unfortunately for him, topped his list. He couldn't put his finger on what made this woman beautiful, though.

Any single feature was lovely, proportioned, balanced,

but not extraordinary, though when they were combined... Perhaps the impression had more to do with the aura of supreme confidence that radiated from her.

Eccentric, too. She wore a black bodysuit paired with a caftan that flowed behind her, brightly colored enough for a circus tent, and had her raven black hair piled in an intricate updo that reminded him of paintings of French royalty in the ostentatious days of Marie Antoinette. Only he got the impression that this woman, who at first glance might appear thirty years old at most, laid claim to an older soul than that. Centuries lurked in her dark eyes. A knowing that immediately set him on the defensive.

"How did you know my name?" he asked, even as he politely grasped her daintily extended hand.

"Delilah called ahead." The woman didn't release his hand. Instead, stepping in to him, she covered their clasped hands with her other one and stared deeply into his eyes. Like she was reading his essence.

"I see," Alasdair said, forcing himself to stand still and endure her inspection. At least Delilah had bothered to do that much. "She failed to provide *your* name."

Lips that reminded him of...someone else, though he couldn't think who...tipped in amusement. "The silly girl."

Not how he would describe Delilah.

"My name is Semhazah. You may call me Hazah."

Why did her full name sound familiar? Something he'd heard before, or perhaps read? He mentally shook that off. How long before they could get to the point?

"So...you have a demon problem?" Hazah asked.

He held in the spurt of surprise that flickered through him and peered closer. Had Delilah sent him to a mind reader? How would that help? Only dark eyes returned his gaze with utter innocence and even a sort of amused tolerance that had him clenching his teeth. He needed all the help he could get.

At least she didn't waste his time with idle chatter, jumping straight in.

"Yes," he bit out.

"Tell me about it."

Quickly he detailed the growing number of incidents and his dealing with Agnes's new situation, which was his proof positive of demons. Hazah, still not releasing his hand, nodded along.

"That *is* concerning," she murmured when he finished.

Alasdair smoothed out the scowl that wanted to furrow his brow. This was like dealing with Delilah. "Concerning is putting it mildly."

She gave a noncommittal hum.

Am I missing something?

The last time demon possessions occurred in these numbers ended up in a trail of events that escalated in horror at the turn of the first millennium. It had taken the combined powers of his people, along with demigods, and even a battalion of angels to eradicate them. Why was he the only one taking this seriously?

"Can you help?" he demanded.

If not, he needed to call the Syndicate together. Now. *That* was where he should be.

Rather than answer, Hazah lifted one beringed hand, a multitude of tinkling bracelets at her wrist, and waved it in front of his face, as though scanning him with her palm. Then she studied him with narrowed eyes. "Fascinating."

What was she doing now? Spock imitations? "What's fasci—"

She grabbed his hand and flipped it palm up, studying it closely. "Oh my. Yes. I see now."

He jerked out of her touch. "Can you help?" he repeated the question, trying not to yell.

Hazah pursed her lips. "I'm afraid Delilah is the only one

who can help you with this."

"She refused," he snapped.

"Is that what happened?" Her tone of voice indicated she didn't entirely believe him. As though he'd be here if it weren't true.

"Yes." *Dammit.* "I just came from there."

Hazah merely shrugged, almost appearing bored. "I guess I'll have to send you right back."

Before he knew what she was about, she whispered a series of words that sounded ominously like a magical spell, but in a dialect he only vaguely recognized. Then she pushed a single, manicured finger into his chest, directly over his heart.

The strangest sensation, like she'd tied a string to that beating organ and yanked hard on the other end, pulled at him, and suddenly he wasn't standing in the gilded marble foyer in her home, but in the office he'd stalked out of not even fifteen minutes ago.

Delilah sat slumped in her chair, elbows propped on her knees and her head in her hands. As his arrival disturbed the papers scattered across her floor, she jerked her head up, pressing a hand over her breast.

Then whipped around to stare in his direction. "Alasdair? What—"

"Your useless *helper* sent me back here," he snapped. "I don't have time for this."

She jerked to her feet and moved around the desk to stand in front of him, tipping her chin up. A glance showed him her shoes were off. Again.

Why am I noticing that right now?

She tracked his glance, spotted her bare feet as well, and went back around her desk to slip her shoes on.

"What is it with you and shoes?" The demand slipped from him. The fact that he asked annoyed him even more.

"Bare feet are more comfortable," she said, coming back around to face him. "But not exactly professional."

Shock skittered through him that she'd answered at all. "Professional is the last thing you need to worry about with me."

"No. With you, I need the added height."

Added height? "What?"

"You're very tall." Now she was speaking through stiff lips, as though reluctant to reveal this.

"And that bothers you? Are you a height-ist? Short people unite?"

"I need any advantage I can get around you." The way she huffed as soon as the words were spoken told him she hadn't meant to reveal that much.

The fact was that those words sent a buzz through him of—what? Not power. More like satisfaction. Which was bad, because his focus should be on his more immediate problem.

"I'm leaving now," he said. "But next time, I promise not to intimidate you if you leave them off."

Earning an annoyed little growl. "You don't intimidate me, jackass."

He struggled to shift with the roller coaster of emotions yanking him around. From protective, to frustrated, to turned-on as hell, to closed down, to pissed, to curious, to amused. "What do I do to you then?"

Damned if he didn't suddenly want the answer to have nothing to do with intimidation. Blood surged south as he waited for the words.

Fuck. What was he doing? "Forget it," he muttered. "Don't answer that."

Her eyebrows shot up, but he ignored her. With jerking motions, Alasdair pulled his cell phone from the inner pocket of his suit jacket and dialed.

"Aluron," Micah answered after one ring.

"I hit a dead end here," he jumped straight into it.

Delilah, meanwhile, was studying him with an impatient frown. Let her wait. She'd wasted his time today. See how she liked it.

He continued issuing his orders. "Convene the Syndicate. See if they can get the demon inside Agnes to talk. Also, have them bring in Rowan Masters. The woman was raised by a demon. Maybe she'll have something. We need information and a plan quickly."

"Understood," Micah said in his ear. No hesitation in his guard's voice. One of his better qualities. "What should I tell your sister?"

"Nothing. Hestia will figure it out when she's called in with the rest of the council members."

"Got it."

"I'll be in touch as soon as I leave here." On that note, he disconnected the call.

"What did Hazah say?" Delilah asked impatiently.

"That only you could help me. Before I could explain that you'd refused, she said something that sounded like a spell, tapped me on the chest, and—"

Shock immobilized his tongue and the rest of him when Delilah reached up with almost frantic fingers and started undoing the buttons of his shirt.

She had three freed before he came back to his senses and brushed her hand away. "What are you doing?"

"Did she leave a mark?"

A mark? He had no idea why he wasn't simply walking out of here. He needed to get home, to his people who didn't know yet what kind of terrible danger they were in. Maybe the urgency in her eyes as she waited for an answer got to him.

Rather than simply leave, he lifted his hands and undid the rest, drawing back his custom-tailored shirt and vest.

Sure enough, a small, star-shaped mark, glowing faintly pink, marred the skin over his heart.

"What the devil?" he muttered.

"This can't be right," Delilah whispered. She lifted her hand and brushed a single finger over the spot.

Instantly, darkness closed in on him. Only he was still lucid. Still aware of his body…and Delilah's. Her touch branding him with unwanted heat that swept through his blood and gathered in his rapidly hardening traitor of a cock. He wrapped a hand around her wrist to tug her off and caught the sound of her gasp in the darkness.

Only he couldn't step away or shake off her hand. As though compelled to keep her touch on him.

"What's happening?" he demanded.

"Damn—"

As fast as the darkness overcame him, it cleared. He blinked in the suddenly harsh light of day. Only, instead of late morning sun, it appeared to be watery light of an overcast afternoon sky, snow drifting down over a forested landscape outside. Instead of Delilah's office with its glassed-in view of the Rocky Mountain peaks behind the downtown Denver skyline, he was standing in what appeared to be a bedroom in a medieval castle—stone walls with thick wood beams, fancy furniture including a massive wood-canopied bed and a carved chest at the foot. Animal-skin rugs of a certain exoticness told him this was a wealthy home.

"Fuck me," Delilah muttered.

The curse on her lips was about the sexiest damn thing he'd ever heard, sending a pulse through his already throbbing dick, a reaction that served only to piss him off more. He glanced down to find he still held her hand against his bare chest.

She noticed at the same time, and slowly stepped away, giving her wrist a tug when he didn't immediately let go.

"Is it me, or are we trapped in some kind of Dr. Who alternate universe kind of thing?" he asked. "Or maybe I'm going to wake up and this is a terrible dream."

Delilah did a rapid blink but didn't answer. Instead, holding his gaze, she opened her mouth and called loudly, "Hazah? What in the seven hells are you doing?"

Immediately, Hazah appeared in the room with them.

Determined to send himself home, over whatever game was being played here, Alasdair flicked his hands open wide, only the magical electricity that was his to command at will didn't condense in his palm like it should. In fact, nothing happened at all. He flicked his hands again. Nothing. A whispered spell resulted in fuck all.

"What have you done?" Alasdair snarled at Hazah, trying not to panic. She'd taken his magic? How was that possible? How was he supposed to protect his people without it?

Hazah gave them both an easy, mysterious smile. "I'm helping, my darlings. You'll see."

Delilah snorted. "How does this help him with his demon—" She cut the word off, rubbing at her wrist through the cuff of her blouse. "With the problem?"

"Don't worry." Hazah flapped a hand. "I'll keep an eye on that while you're occupied."

Occupied? "Occupied doing what?" Alasdair demanded, drawing himself up and setting a demanding stare on her that had cowed greater men and women than her. He assumed greater. Actually, he still didn't know what she was.

"I've arranged a little trip for you. Some things you both need to see if you're going to get through tonight." Spoken as though they hadn't a care in the world.

"Are you kidding me?" Delilah practically growled the words between clenched teeth. "Your timing is for shit."

A small, removed part of him had to admit to being impressed. At least he wasn't the only one pissed about this.

Hazah didn't even blink. "I've bound you together for this journey, and where you are, magic doesn't work, so don't even bother to try, Mr. Blakesley." Hazah flicked a glance at his hands, limp at his sides now. "Enjoy."

With a frilly wave, their "helper" disappeared.

Alasdair turned to find Delilah standing with her eyes screwed shut, muttering to herself.

"Want to explain that?" he demanded. "I have a fucking demon problem to deal with."

Her eyes snapped open, and, for a heartbeat, he swore contrition gazed back at him before she composed herself. "I know, but from past experience, there's nothing we can do. Let's just get through this quickly."

"The hell with that. I'm leaving."

"How?" she demanded.

Alasdair ground his teeth together. He was in a castle, which meant he was far away from California where his people were, so walking his ass out of here was not an option. And his magic wasn't working.

"This is…" He shook his head, too furious to put words to it.

"I know not being in charge of *this*"—she waved a hand between them—"is difficult. Especially for a man who apparently needs to control everything around him. When I first met you, I assumed it was a bit of a Napoleon complex."

"I'm six-three—"

Her lips tipped in a Cheshire smile. "I didn't mean short by that reference."

Napoleon complex, but not because he was small. So, what? He was a power-hungry tyrant?

He scowled. It better not be the other small reference.

"I mean, I understand the need for control, of course. It's…necessary."

Alasdair tried to switch gears from the irritation of being

compared to a tyrant to being placated for that facet of his personality, all while an imp of a smile peeked at him from the most unexpected source.

Weeding through all that, his mind glommed onto the word "necessary." A telling descriptor. As though she knew that truth for herself. Made sense. He'd known the first time they'd met that he was staring at a mirror image of himself. He searched for a response to any part of this conversation, or to her in general.

"Listen up, goddess," he snapped. "You got us into this, sending me to her. Now you get us out."

"It doesn't work like that." Seemingly oblivious to his reaction, Delilah continued blithely on. "But I promise, when it's over, while I can't help you directly, I'll hand over every resource I have at my disposal for your use."

He crossed his arms and glared at her. Apparently he had no choice here. "What do we have to do?"

. . .

Delilah folded her hands in front of her, trying to project calm, even as she dug her bare toes into the thick wool of the achingly familiar bearskin rug covering the cold stone floor. These visions always felt so damn real and yet not at the same time.

Damn her mother to one of the seven hells. Preferably the third one. Hazah hated that one the most.

Alasdair wasn't far off with that random, and unexpected, *Dr. Who* reference. Who knew the man had any association with pop culture of the human variety? She'd sort of assumed that, like the goddess Athena, he'd sprung to life a fully formed adult who'd eschew such common pursuits.

"She did this to me as a child." Actually, multiple times over the course of her life, but he didn't need to know that.

"Did what, exactly?" The man was practically vibrating with anger.

Trapped in a nightmare with a pissed-off warlock of incredible power was not where she wanted to be. Even if he couldn't access his magic.

The happy giggle of a child behind them had them both jerking around.

A little girl of not more than three knelt on the cold stone floor in front of the fireplace. She hadn't been there a second ago. Adorned in a dress of fine material with intricate embroidery at the hem and sleeves, but with bare feet, her black hair curling down her back, she petted Penelope, her cat. An early Christmas present from her father.

"It starts now," Delilah said.

Alasdair jerked his gaze to her. "What is going on?"

Forcing herself to look up, she grimaced. "You know Dickens' classic story, *A Christmas Carol*?"

He crossed his arms, muscles stretching the fine material of his jacket, spreading his undone shirt farther apart. Seriously, the man had to have some physical flaw, though darned if she'd found one yet. "What does that have to do with this?" he asked.

Not the easiest thing to explain. "Hazah gave Dickens the idea for that story. She likes to use that trick to teach people...lessons."

Alasdair didn't so much as move a hair on his beautiful head, but disbelief became palpable. "You're telling me we're about to be visited by the ghosts of the past, present, and future?"

"Well...it *is* Christmas Eve," she pointed out wryly. "But no. Not ghosts, exactly. More like lucid visions."

"To what end?"

She blew out a long breath, the visible show of emotion uncharacteristic for her. "Choices and consequences," she said. "When Hazah sees a future, she can see pieces of what lead up to it, like stepping-stones. She shows you that path."

"Why?"

Delilah shrugged. In the past, it had always been a future where she'd broken the oath she'd made as a child. Clearly not what was happening here. "With the hope that you change the future she saw coming."

Alasdair blew out a breath. "Why can't she just tell me how to change the future she saw?"

"Because she doesn't know. All she can see is the ending coming if you stay on your current path, not what happens if things change."

"I don't believe this." He ran a hand over his jaw.

"I know. I'm sorry." Her lips twisted. "Hopefully, this is about your demon problem. A clue as to how to deal with it or what actions result in a worse situation."

He ran that same hand around the back of his neck. "I should have known coming to you was a mistake."

Ouch. His words struck deep, lodging under her skin in a way that she shouldn't allow. She owed this man nothing. Besides, she *was* trying to help, in her limited capacity.

"There's no way out of it and no way to stop beyond going through what she wants us to see."

Please, Mother, no revealed secrets.

She didn't need this powerful man holding those over her.

Chapter Three

Alasdair was still contemplating a response when a high-pitched scream shattered the quiet that fell between them. Not the happy squeal of a girl at play. Instead, the heartrending cry of a child's brokenness. They both looked down, only now the child version of herself was bent over the cat.

"I didn't mean to," Delilah whispered along with the child version of herself.

The pain in grown-up Delilah's voice about took Alasdair's knees out from under him. An inexplicable reaction when he was still fucking furious about being stuck here.

But he knew for certain, after their encounters this year, that she didn't share her emotions with others. Took one to know one. That she couldn't hide her pain from him, while she watched what was apparently the young version of herself, got to him. Like a thousand needles in his skin.

Child Delilah lifted her face to the heavens, cheeks red and blotchy and drenched in tears. "I didn't mean to. I didn't mean to."

The little girl's plea made that needle sensation only worse. Alasdair crouched beside the cat and even reached out to put a hand to its belly to make sure the animal was dead. With a jerk, he stopped himself short, realizing this had already happened. He couldn't fix it for her.

"What did you do?" Alasdair lifted his head to ask the woman standing back from the scene, arms wrapped around her middle.

She didn't pull her gaze from the cat, or maybe she couldn't. "My powers got away from me. I was trying to train her to play dead, like a dog. A surprise for my father, who never liked cats. Only—" She swallowed hard, a shudder visibly passing through her.

Fuck. He might not be able to help the child, but he *could* help the woman. Even if she didn't deserve it. Alasdair got to his feet and deliberately stood in front of her, blocking her view. "Don't watch."

She lifted her head. Gaze dull, dazed, she seemed to stare through him, so self-contained, it hurt to watch.

Why was this bothering him so much? He'd hardened his heart to witnessing others in pain or peril long ago. A man in his position would be driven mad by the numbers of lost souls if he didn't find a way to compartmentalize. Usually he could. He'd gotten good at it, given his childhood.

Why not now? Why not with her?

Jaw clenched against the sight of the sorrow clearly ripping her apart, Alasdair took her by the shoulders. "Look at me."

She focused on him with dark eyes so shadowed they appeared bruised.

"It already happened," he said. "It's over. You don't have to go through it again."

She blinked slowly, and an emotion flitted across her face that he didn't quite catch. Dread, if he had to hazard a guess.

"It's not over yet," the woman he shielded whispered.

"I can make repairs," the child version of herself said at the same time.

Still blocking grown-up Delilah's view, not letting go of her, Alasdair glanced over his shoulder to find the girl holding her hands over the cat. A soft glow came from her palms as she whispered words—vaguely familiar words tickling at his memory—over the body. The glow grew brighter, building and ebbing, and then the cat gave a shaky meow.

"Impossible," Alasdair whispered. He knew of no magic that could raise the dead.

"Penelope." The child cried and gathered the now very live cat into her arms, rubbing her tears against its white fur.

"Lily?" a male voice called out, the urgent edge reflected in the man's face as he hurried into the room. Dressed in the fashion of medieval court, tall and muscled, he could have passed for one of the gods with his blond hair, bronzed skin, and bright blue eyes.

"Your father?" Alasdair slid a glance to Delilah, who nodded.

"What is he?" he asked next.

But she only stood there, mute and still. Which meant more was coming.

The man took in the cat and the girl's tears in a single glance. "What did you do?" he whispered through lips gone chalky white.

"I healed her, Papa." Dimples appeared in rounded, still wet cheeks, as the girl offered a proud grin and held the cat out to her father.

An expression that was more terror than wonder seized her father's face, and Delilah herself closed her eyes against the sight.

"What's going to happen?" Alasdair asked.

"It cannot be time," her father whispered, the words

hoarse in his throat, as though arguing with himself. "She is only a baby, yet."

Three years old at the most. Unconsciously, Alasdair tightened his grip on the adult version. "Time for what?"

"To bind my powers."

"What? No." That could be incredibly dangerous, locking energy inside a child.

If magic wasn't expunged regularly, it could result in catastrophic explosions or madness or other horrible ends. Was this why she'd refused to help? Because she had no access to her powers? Was this what Hazah wanted him to see? That the choice to go to Delilah in the first place had been the wrong one because she couldn't help?

But that made no sense, because she could have gotten anyone on her payroll to help instead. Her business was about helping people.

She did go to someone else, a small voice reminded him. Otherwise they wouldn't be here right now.

"Delilah," her father said to the girl, going down on one knee and gathering her to him. "Do you remember the words we've been practicing?"

Her puckered brow an unconscious imitation of her father's expression, the tiny girl nodded.

"It's time to mean the words, my darling. As an unbreakable oath."

Tears welled in wide dark eyes, her lower lip trembling. "Mama does not wish for this. She said—"

"I know." Her father pulled her in to him. "But your mama can't be here. I do not wish this either, but we have no choice. They will come for you if we don't."

"Who?" Alasdair asked, though he didn't pull his gaze away. "Who will come?"

Still gripping her by the arms, he didn't miss the way Delilah shifted in his grip. He turned to face her as she crept her hands up over her ears. "Don't watch," she whispered.

Her father began to chant, and the child, mimicking her parent, repeated a string of words, again in that known-yet-unknown language. Over and over, until suddenly she tipped her head back and screamed, even louder than before.

Thrashing in her father's arms, the child clawed at the skin around her wrists, which turned red and blistered as Alasdair watched in horror. Through it all, her father didn't relent, continuing to chant.

"Stop! Stop!" the child screamed. "It burns."

"God's above," Alasdair whispered.

A tremor shook the woman he still gripped, and he pulled her in to his chest. Wrapping one arm around her, he tucked her head into the crook of his neck with the other hand at the back of her head, entwined in silky hair, no doubt disturbing the elegant styling. He held her as she whimpered through every blood-curdling second as the child version of her screamed in agony.

"It'll be over soon," he murmured into her hair but didn't let her go. Not when she was shaking hard enough to rattle his teeth. He wasn't that much of an asshole. Or maybe it had *some*thing to do with her...and him. But he wasn't about to take that truth out and examine it any closer.

"No," the woman in his arms moaned. "It's not over yet."

The words and the torment wrapped up in them pierced through layers he'd built over the years. Layers meant to keep him separate, keep him safe from the world. From others.

"Hell," he muttered.

Taking her face in his hands, he lifted her chin. "Look at me."

Delilah's eyes fluttered open, dark eyes hazy. Miserable. Need reflected back at him. A silent plea to make this stop. Only he didn't know how. His magic wasn't accessible here. He'd tried.

Another screech from the child and Delilah scrunched her eyes closed. "Dammit." Alasdair did the only thing he could think of. He brought his lips down over hers, claiming her lush mouth—something he'd fantasized about for months—in a desperate attempt to distract them both.

Beneath his touch, Delilah froze at the sudden contact. He expected her to pull away, maybe even knee him in the groin. She didn't do either. Instead, her breathing hitched, then she melted into him, opening under his mouth, letting him in.

Mother goddess. He hardly noticed the sudden silence that surrounded them, too absorbed by the woman in his arms.

The kiss changed from hard possession, softening, slowing. The taste of cherries—sweet and tart—only added to the need growing within him. He savored her flavor and her small sighs. Sliding his hands down her arms, he wrapped his own around her, bringing her body up against his more fully, the scent of flowers surrounding him.

And she was there with him every step along the way, wrapping her arms around his neck, trying to get closer, sighs changing to whimpers. Not close enough.

This isn't about me, a small voice whispered, bringing with it guilt on wings of forbearance This was about her. Protecting her from her past.

Forcing himself to stop, he slid his hands to her waist, meaning to set her back, step away. He even lifted his head. Only she went up on tiptoe, those soft warm lips chasing his, pulling him back in. This wasn't what he'd meant to do, where he'd meant to take them. He should have enough control over himself to end this.

Instead, he balanced at the edge of need, ready to topple over into an abyss of wanting that he should be fighting. He shouldn't be here.

She nipped at his lower lip, and Alasdair groaned, gathering her close again. Plundering her mouth, her body shifting against him in what had to be an unconsciously given invitation. Delilah would never allow herself that kind of vulnerability. Not with him, especially.

The realization gave him the strength he needed to lift his head. Jerk it up, more like. The actions of a desperate man.

The silence finally penetrated.

They still stood in her room in her castle home. Alone. The ghosts of her past gone. Not even the crackle of the fire disturbing the peace.

Then blackness. Like before.

All-consuming, although he could still feel Delilah in his arms. Stiffer now. The vulnerability from a second ago—in a way he never in a thousand years would have expected from her—gone. He didn't need to be able to see her face to know she was regretting that kiss. Her body telegraphed that fact to him.

The blackness lifted as suddenly as it had descended. Only this time revealing a nighttime scene, and Alasdair stared at the familiar home they stood outside—aglow with strings of Christmas lights all along the roofline—his own dread descending like being buried alive, his heart thudding harder against his ribs.

No.

The word broke inside his head, and he had to swallow back the bile burning as it rose up his throat. Even though he still owned it, he'd never wanted to see this place again.

Gods, he should have guessed.

Tension rolled through him, gripping his muscles, stringing them so tightly, Delilah shifted against him on a murmured protest. Then stilled.

He could feel her stare, the questions rising in her. "Where are we?" she asked.

"Apparently it's my turn."

• • •

The man had kissed every lucid thought from her mind in the middle of the worst moment of her life and sent her body into a spiral of sensation that still gripped her like nothing before in her long, long life. Madness. Only she couldn't think about that right now, because if Alasdair tensed any more, he'd snap like an Achilles tendon bearing too much strain. His expression one she could only describe as haunted.

Delilah glanced around them, wondering at the source of his sudden unease. They stood surrounded by mountains, towering sentinels in the dark. Snow on the ground, which oddly they couldn't feel inside the vision beyond a general sense of cold. In front of them stood a massive mountain cabin that seemed to have been built around two sides of a large, clear pond. Moonlight illuminated the scene from outside while a warm glow from lamps inside beckoned her closer.

"Your turn?"

"What could I possibly have to learn from this?" he muttered.

"Hey." A hand to his cheek and some gentle pressure and Alasdair turned to look down at her. "What is this?" she asked.

"This is the night my father killed my entire family. All but me, and my youngest sister, Hestia, who wasn't there." He said the words so matter-of-factly, it took her a moment to absorb their meaning.

His entire family… "I'm so sorry."

Bright blue eyes suddenly blazed with an emotion she doubted he ever let anyone else see. Trepidation.

Her own horrible memories melted away, and she focused

on him.

"I assume this won't be over until we witness the memory?" he asked.

Dammit, Mother. Delilah gave a reluctant nod.

"Come on, then." Grabbing her by the hand, they walked across a small bridge that spanned a burbling, ice-crusted stream, along a snow-lined gravel path to the house, and right in through the open front door. Open because it hung off the hinges, she could now see.

There they found a scene of absolute horror. Chaos reigned, as though a hurricane had blown through the room, furniture scattered, festive holiday decorations shredded, windows blown out on the wall facing away from the pond, and crimson blood, still wet, splashed across the walls.

So much blood.

No bodies. Thank heavens.

Amid the chaos, on a loveseat obviously re-righted, because it had been set at an odd angle in the room, sat a boy of maybe eight—black hair, blue eyes, and a strength in him even then that revealed itself in a hard-set jaw. Not a tear in sight. He kept clenching his hands, bright bands of electricity wrapping and slithering about his fists, almost as though he was playing with his power.

"So young?" Delilah asked. Most mages came into their powers at puberty.

The man still holding her hand, though she was sure he wasn't aware, nodded, lips set in a grim slash. "My powers manifested in full that night."

A group of men and women—mages at a guess, though difficult to tell when she couldn't feel the crackle of their energy in this dreamscape—gathered in one corner of the room murmured in low voices she couldn't hear. Which meant he hadn't heard that night, either, almost as though he hadn't wanted to, because they'd been standing close enough.

They kept glancing over at him, expressions full of concern and…fear.

A witch, her gunmetal gray hair pinned in a knot at the nape of her neck, separated from them to sit beside Alasdair. "The Syndicate has ruled your use of underage magic to be in self-defense."

The boy said nothing. If anything, though he turned his head, he looked straight through her. She might as well have not been there at all.

Then he cradled his arm in a protective move and Delilah had to hold back a gasp at the raw, burned skin visible along one side of his skinny little appendage. Had no one seen to his wounds? Checked that he was physically harmed?

Delilah wanted to wrap that self-contained boy up in her arms and tell him everything was going to be fine and perform a healing spell all at the same time. Couldn't these people see how much he was hurting? Physically, yes. But even more so emotionally. How he hid his pain behind the numb blankness? Instead, she tightened her grip on the man's hand.

Alasdair dragged his gaze away from the younger version of himself to look at her. A question in his eyes that he didn't voice.

"Whatever you survived…remember how far you've come since then," she said.

His bright blue gaze narrowed, turning intense and chasing a sensation through her that was this side of inappropriate, ill-timed, unwanted need. Her skin prickled, awareness surging, and desire gathering.

Wrong in every way.

But then his eyes went glacial, so like the boy version of himself, as though he deliberately was freezing her out. "You don't even know what I did."

Delilah released his hand, though she wouldn't allow

herself to step back. "I don't have to. You're the leader of the Covens Syndicate now. That wouldn't happen if what you did was wrong."

"Wrong?" His lips pulled back in an expression nearly feral. "No. Not...wrong."

The woman on the couch leaned forward, apparently trying to get through to the younger Alasdair. "Your father was possessed by a demon," she said.

A demon.

Deep cold stole through Delilah, freezing out the warmth lingering from his look, freezing her emotions at the same time. She glanced around the room more closely until she found the spot. In the corner, the plaster of the wall was destroyed in a spiderweb of cracks and blackened as though charred by a thunderbolt.

She turned her head to stare at the man. Alasdair had killed a demon that young? One possessing his own father, too?

Fuck me.

Of course it *would* have to be a demon.

Damn. What was her mother thinking tying her to this man? Nothing they could learn was going to allow her to help him, no matter what.

Damn her inability to See when it came to him. If she'd known...

She'd assumed, when she'd first realized her blind spot when it came to Alasdair, that it meant their futures weren't linked. Now, with one fell swoop, her mother had changed all that.

"You had no choice," the witch said to the boy. "There's no shame in it."

"You think I'm *ashamed*?" the boy asked in a tone of voice so like the man, Delilah's lips parted in a silent gasp. "I'm not ashamed. I'm—" He shook his head, then gave the woman the same cold stare he'd just given Delilah. "My family is dead."

The witch got to her feet, stepping back, expression saying even more than the distance she put between them that she had no idea how to react to that. "I'm sorry," she said after a brief hesitation.

Both boy and man scoffed. "I'm sure you are," the boy said. The electricity wrapped around his hands crackled and snapped.

"Oh, Alasdair," Delilah whispered.

She may as well have yelled it, the way he flinched. Then he snapped his gaze to her, brows lowered in a fierce glare that didn't fool her one bit. "I don't need your pity or your apologies. You had nothing to do with it."

Despite the horrible scenario playing out before them, Delilah couldn't help the stupidly inappropriate twitch of her lips. "*Pity* is the last thing I'd ever feel for *you*, Alasdair Blakesley."

Not even for the child on the couch. Heartache, maybe, but never pity.

The way his stiff shoulders eased minutely told her he'd understood.

"These people are fools," she said, shocked at the vehemence in her own voice. "Please tell me someone knew enough to give you a hug that day, help you through this."

He turned his head, searching her expression. "Is that what you would have done?"

Delilah bit her lip, but that didn't stop the truth from spilling out anyway, because deep down she sensed he needed to hear this. "I'd hug you now if you'd let me."

Breath punched from him in an audible puff, though his expression didn't change. Then he gave his head a shake, as if deciding what to believe. Part of her hoped he'd relent. That he would allow himself to take some belated comfort, even if he didn't like her. That all-consuming kiss notwithstanding.

He didn't do that, though. Instead, Alasdair tipped his head back to shout at the ceiling. "That's enough."

Nothing happened.

Was there more her mother wanted them to witness? Wouldn't he know if there were more?

A spot over her heart, where no doubt a mark matching the one Alasdair bore, warmed until it became uncomfortable, and Delilah silently cursed her parent.

"I think you have to take my hand," she said, and held hers out.

He stared at her as if she'd grown a few extra heads, then reached for her.

But Delilah jerked away with a gasp.

"I'm not going to hurt you—"

She waved him off, still staring at what had caught her attention. Leaving Alasdair standing there, she walked closer to the boy on the couch, right up to him, and bent over.

There.

In the center of his forehead, a slight red glow that faded even more as she watched. Delilah squeezed her eyes shut for a second. Holy hells, had none of the witches and warlocks in the room seen this mark that night?

She blinked, then froze as the younger Alasdair had lifted his gaze. This was the past, and she couldn't influence it, but she swore he was looking directly at her. Impossible.

Giving herself a shake, she straightened and turned to the man. "You were marked."

He frowned, his gaze dropping to the boy. "Marked?"

"That night. A demon, usually an upper level one, had been assigned to possess you. There is always a reason." Always. "And until they achieve what they're after, they don't stop trying, which likely explains your current predicament."

Alasdair crossed his arms. "I killed it."

She shook her head. "If you'd killed it, the mark wouldn't be there. You killed its underling."

She didn't blame him for the way he frowned, denial stark in his eyes. She wouldn't want to believe such a thing, either. "What does this mean?"

"I'm not sure yet. Best guess? This demon attack and the ones happening now are connected. They want you for a reason. Can you think of anything a demon might want?"

The spot over her heart warmed again, suddenly.

His must've as well, because he grimaced. "I guess we dissect this later."

He was right. The faster they got through the visions, the sooner he could return to his people. Delilah crossed back to his side and held out her hand, which he took in a distracted way, most likely thinking through what she'd just said, his hand swallowing hers whole.

Instantly, the darkness consumed her vision, her only link to reality the strong, remarkably steady hand wrapped around her own.

Chapter Four

Sight returned in a blink and a shiver over his skin, though Alasdair recognized that he wasn't actually feeling the cold. More like the idea of the cold, the memory. Snow again. Just a dusting of it this time, crystalizing on the tops of storefront awnings and parked cars.

Delilah slipped her hand from his. In the transition, he forgot he hadn't wanted to touch her again. Contrarily, he didn't want to let go now.

She'd been a beacon of warmth, of escape, in the middle of that memory—of that moment he'd tried so hard to block out and forget since the night he'd left the house for good. The edge of that memory had been dulled, though. Almost like her presence today had altered it somehow. Reached through the past and made it…not easier exactly—

Focus. If he couldn't be in the here and now, dealing with a demon problem, then he'd damn well use his time wisely.

Since, apparently, he'd been marked to be a target for all of time. Why him? Was taking over mages, with the variety of powers, always the plan, and he'd just been caught in the crossfire as a youth? Or was it the fact he came from an ancient magical family line and was extremely powerful? Maybe that was why they'd gone after his father initially—he'd been the head of the Covens Syndicate at the time.

But did they need Alasdair for his power? Or to keep him from preventing their uprising?

Had he been the one to bring the demon problem down on his own people?

The familiarity of the street where they now stood settled over him like déjà vu. Thankfully, not in the same gut-wrenching way his childhood home had. Sparkling red and green Christmas decorations adorned the streetlamps and storefronts and signs advertised holiday sales. Familiar Christmas carols piped from several of the stores as patrons opened the doors.

Clearly this was his memory they were visiting. A theme was starting to form here. Both of their previous memories had happened around the holidays. Did she despise this time of year as much as he did?

"Come on," she said, then took off down the street, obviously having an idea of what was going on. Only...why would she?

With a frown he hurried to catch up, long strides bringing him to her side quickly. "This is *my* memory," he said. "Shouldn't I be leading?"

She flicked him a wary glance. "I'm pretty sure this one is mine."

Alasdair stopped her with a hand to her elbow. "It can't be. After...my family's death, I went to live with my aunt and uncle in New York. I walked this street almost every day between school and their home." He'd refused the chauffeur.

Dark eyes searched his. Delilah was back in control of herself, not betraying her thoughts by so much as a blink.

He didn't like it.

In the same way he didn't like it when the ending of a book didn't meet with his expectations. Or when demons showed up and started possessing his people. It couldn't be because he'd liked seeing the softer side of her. The side that had welcomed his hold, his comfort. The sense of… connection…to the real woman behind the façade.

"Don't do that," he said.

She blinked, a crease forming between her brows. "Do what?"

"Wall me out."

"I'm not."

He leaned over to look closely into her eyes. "Yeah. The bricks are going up faster than I thought." He straightened, fighting the ridiculous urge to grin at her aggrieved glare. He'd rather she be angry than shut off. "Like it or not, we're partners in this."

"I know that," she snapped.

"Good."

She threw up her hands. "Great."

They both settled, gazes locked, and damned if heat didn't flare through him. Gods, he *wanted* her. A bad idea no matter what angle he looked at it from. Maybe antagonizing her was a bad idea.

"You're sure?" she asked, breaking his thoughts into fragments. "About this being yours?"

He took a second to pick back up on the conversation. "Yes."

"Then how would I know that the next vision is going to happen down here?" She turned him by the shoulders, and Alasdair stilled.

He recognized this alley.

Darker than others, full of boxes and piles of trash bags. As a kid, he'd gotten a creepy feeling about it, though he refused to avoid it. And a good thing, too, because—

Eighteen-year-old him came strolling down the street and passed right through current day him, sending a sickening sensation rolling through his stomach. But the memory of himself stopped suddenly, staring into the darkness of the alley. Listening.

Alasdair already knew for what.

. . .

Delilah had no doubt exactly what came next. The windigo she'd defeated. Horrible creatures, and she'd only ever come across the one. This had been a job she hadn't contracted out to any of her people, taking it on herself, because of a promise she'd made to a phoenix in exchange for a favor. But what the hell did that have to do with Alasdair?

She peered closer at the boy standing before them. Almost a man, balanced at the beginning of adult life, though his blue eyes had held a sadness that day. Something deeper than what a kid that age should know.

Black hair. Crystal blue eyes. Cut glass jaw. The same aura of total command.

With a silent gasp, she swung her head sharply to stare at Alasdair, picturing him younger, his features not yet as sharp as they were, hair floppier, shoulders not as broad.

"Oh my gods. That was *you*?"

That had Alasdair snapping his head around to stare at her with eyes narrowed then opening wide on a wave of realization. "What do you mean?"

Before she could answer, a gurgling sound, like someone trying to inhale through water without a snorkel, came from deep in the alley, and the younger version of Alasdair took off, running directly toward danger.

Instead of following, though, Delilah suddenly found herself in the back of the alley, her perspective changed.

Blinking at the suddenness of the transition, she lifted arms clothed differently—a long-sleeved black shirt and skintight pants in a soft, easily maneuverable spandex material. Leather boots on her feet, good for running for a fast escape. She'd worn a black cloak that day, the hood up, hair braided over one shoulder.

I'm inside my own body. Her mother had never done this before. Was she going to relive the moment inside herself?

Where was Alasdair?

Only she didn't have time to search. That gurgling sound was a man, and the beast at his throat was one of the more gruesome sights she'd encountered in her long life. The thing she was after had already started a fresh kill before she could get there. But if she could stop it now, the human might live.

Gathering her power inside herself, she knew she had only one shot at this before the windigo turned on her. Larger, faster, and with the ability to paralyze its victims with one bite, it could kill her before she could protect herself or escape if she wasn't careful. She opened her mouth to whisper the words to manifest the power to obliterate the creature. Words taught to her by both her parents.

She lifted her hands, ready to unleash.

"Get off him!" the boy demanded, voice deeper than one would expect from a teenager. More than a hint of the man to come.

Carefully, trying not to draw attention to herself, Delilah stepped back into the shadows.

The windigo, still unaware of her presence, rose from the human it was gnawing on, and the boy's startlingly blue eyes tracked it up and up and up. Over twelve feet of towering beast. The thing had the head of a deer, antlers spreading wide from the top, but all bone, like staring at a skull bleached white by the sun. Black sockets where the eyes and nose should be. But what made her flinch, a rare bout of revulsion bubbling up inside her, was the fact that it had no skin anywhere. Its bones and the red sinews of its muscles were exposed.

Legend had it, a windigo lived in constant agony in this form.

It relied on human flesh to skin itself. To see. The longer it went between meals, the more of its body rotted away. The putrid scent of it filled the alley, overwhelming the already sour scent of the trash.

Suddenly Delilah caught it—not Delilah from the original moment, but herself now. The faint glow of the demon's mark on Alasdair's forehead. She jerked her focus to the creature. Without eyes in its sockets, it was impossible to tell. Was the thing possessed?

It must be, because that mark would glow like that only around the demon who'd marked Alasdair. It had come for him again. This time in the body of a monster. A supernatural creature who was pure instinct. No reasoning, just killing. Demons loved to possess creatures such as those.

Except, if the demon had marked him, he was out to possess him, not kill him. She jerked her head around, searching.

There.

In the darkest recesses of the alley, a column of smoke the size of a man lurked in the shadows. Waiting. How many other demon attacks had he survived? And why were they so intent on taking Alasdair?

Shit. We're in trouble. She paused at the thought and mentally corrected. *He* was in trouble, and she could do nothing but stand by and watch. A thought that sat like sludge in her gut, oozing through her.

What else had she missed that day? Delilah focused on the moment, re-experiencing everything as her old self went through the motions.

The boy Alasdair didn't step back as the monster stalked

him. Instead he raised his chin, staring the thing down. Then white-blue electricity ignited in his palms, forming ropes around his hands as he curled them into fists.

The windigo, sensing power in this new, fresh meat, abandoned the poor man lying unconscious and oozing blood on a heap of rubbish, and stalked toward the boy, head bobbing lightly as it sized up its prey.

Damn.

Delilah stepped out of the shadows. "You don't want him," she said in a cajoling voice. "I promise, I have more power than a child."

The windigo whipped toward the sound of her voice, lifting its nose—exposed bone with a hole where the flesh should be—to sniff the air.

"Lady, run. I have this," the boy insisted.

"Not if you knew what this is," she tossed back, keeping her eyes on the creature who'd stilled between them.

"What is it?"

"A windigo."

"The flesh eaters? I thought they were extinct?"

"Apparently not."

Again, Delilah gathered her power inside her. This type of creature, malevolence incarnate, wouldn't die by physical means. She needed to send its spirit to the hell reserved for evil. She needed to guide it into the runes she'd already drawn on the ground. A trap that would funnel it where she wanted. This would've been a lot easier to do with surprise on her side. Dammit.

Wind whipped down the alley, stirring papers and loose trash, sending it swirling around the creature. Sensing where that power was coming from now, it turned away from the boy, stalking toward her. Delilah backed up carefully, focused on the words, on the power. It should be slowing down, given what she was throwing at it. But it wasn't. Instead it kept coming at her, fast.

She scurried to keep out of reach, while trying to get it to move to its right a few feet. Except the focus she needed to perform this complicated of a ritual was slowing down her physical reaction times. A mistake she realized the second the thing swiped at her with its extra-long arm, backhanding her hard. Delilah hit the brick of the building wall, her head ringing with the crack of sound from the impact, then dropped to her side.

"I've got it!" The boy's voice penetrated the stunned stupor clouding her mind.

She sat up to find those electric lines wrapping around the windigo, keeping it from coming any closer to her, though it strained against the bindings.

"Pull it to the right!" she yelled.

Somehow, face contorted with determination, the boy managed to shift the massive creature. The second it entered her circle, the lines on the ground lit up, as though glowing from underneath.

Seeing her opening, Delilah leaped to her feet and continued chanting, calling upon magic as ancient as the universe itself. The winds whipped harder and the windigo howled like a hyena, high-pitched and creepy. One of the electric lines snapped, and it surged closer, struggling against the boy's bonds, reaching for her with taloned fingers.

"I can't hold it much longer," he called, still out of sight, blocked by the body of the creature they were working together to destroy.

Delilah whispered the last of the words.

The windigo's scream changed pitch, turning frenetic as the thing shook from antlers to bony feet. Then the rest of its body disintegrated, one piece at a time. The screeching was the last thing to go, cut off abruptly.

But did we kill the demon inside the creature? Or just

send it back to the hells?

The wind ceased the instant it was gone, and suddenly the original Delilah faced the boy across a divide of darkened alley, a dusting of snow falling over them, both of them breathing heavily.

A glance in that back corner, and the demon was gone already.

The old her was still catching her breath, and tossed him a smile. "You did good, kid."

"I'm not a kid," he said. Not cocky or whiny. Just stating a fact.

Delilah tipped her head, regarding him more closely. "No. I can see you've been a man longer than your age would indicate."

He drew his shoulders back. "I had no choice."

That deep, aching sadness lingered in the tones. Only *now* Delilah knew what he meant. She'd witnessed the aftermath. Watched a young boy try to contain his hurt and fear and the fact that his world had been ripped apart while no one helped him cope. Not really.

A flash of images hit her mind, as sometimes happened with her ability to See.

Oh my gods. She'd forgotten all about that small prediction that day.

It had happened so fast, been so simple. And nothing that required her intervention. Images of the boy as a man. Gaining more and more magical power. Taking an important position among his people. Doing great things—selfless things, for the sake of his kind.

"I foresee a future of leadership for you," she heard the words coming from her own mouth, even as the memory resounded in her mind. "You'll become a helper to those who need it most. A protector. A good man. Don't let anyone or anything tell you otherwise."

She nodded at the human, out cold but still bleeding. "For now...help him."

Before the boy could take a step closer, she whispered another series of words, these faster and easier than the spell to vanquish the windigo, and disappeared.

In the same instant, she found her current self back outside that alley, standing beside Alasdair the man. He turned to her, face like a granite wall, unreadable. "That was *you*."

Not a question this time. More like an accusation.

"I didn't know," she said. "I promise I didn't know that was you."

"But you saw my future," he insisted, a note in his voice off. Too intense. Too...something.

She shook her head. "I saw flashes. Results. More than I saw you. Or I would have recognized you when we met... formally."

His thick brows lowered over eyes still intensely blue. But he nodded slowly, seeming to accept her word. "You were in the dark, with that hood over your head," he murmured, gaze skating over her features. "I never saw your face."

"I—" But what else could she say. Delilah stared back, waiting. Waiting for him to say something else or drop it or look away. Or for the blackness to return and take them somewhere new. What else in this moment could her mother possibly need them to understand?

"You changed my life that day," Alasdair said in a voice gone gruff. Red flags of color appeared over his cheekbones, the skin drawing tight. "That prediction...it made me who I am today."

A dizzying rush of—Pride? Thankfulness? Neither made sense—waylaid her, and Delilah had to force herself not to look away. "I didn't make you who you are, Alasdair," she said quietly. "It was always there, that potential future.

Always part of you. I just told you not to doubt it."

A protector. The prediction rattled around inside her. A *good* man. A rare person she could put her trust in.

I wish to all the gods I could help you.

"Did you ever think of me after that?"

The quiet question caught her raw.

"Sometimes." She smiled. "I wondered what had become of that boy. If he'd turned into the man I'd seen in those flashes."

Hell, he'd become so much more based not just on her research of him recently, but on what today had revealed. On the way he'd held her when she'd been hurting, even as angry as he was with her. The way his concern for his people was almost palpable in his frustration to get through this.

The way her body came to life with every damn touch.

Alasdair stepped in to her, framing her face with his hands, sending sparks of need along the sensitive nerves of her skin, his blue eyes so intense her heart ratcheted up, electricity singing through her blood and wakening a part of her that only he seemed able to bring to life.

With that kiss. Now with a simple look.

"I'm not a boy anymore," he said, import in every syllable.

Then, holding her gaze, he slowly lowered his lips over hers. But he paused before he touched her and she found herself swaying in to him, reaching for him.

"I thought of you," he whispered, a heartbeat before pressing a soft kiss to her lips.

Chapter Five

Who the hell knew that nirvana came with the taste of cherries and the softest lips?

Or that what felt like a hundred years after fighting beside that mystery woman in the alley, Alasdair would be truly a man in his own right, master of his domain, and kissing that woman here. Because damned if he hadn't wanted to kiss her again since the first time.

He'd dreamed of her…for years.

Delilah didn't passively accept his kisses. She leaned in to him, fingers spiking through his hair, kneading his scalp like a cat, making small noises that sent him into hyperdrive. Passion and perfection in his arms. None of that icy control when he touched her, almost as though there were two halves to her.

That she let him this close, let him see this other side fully, a hell of a lot more than the glimpses she'd inadvertently given him before now, reached inside his chest and cracked him wide open.

A fact that should scare the everliving fuck out of him,

but he was too far down the rabbit hole to care right this second. Caught up in his fascination. Not wanting to miss a second.

Delilah gave a shuddering sigh as he slid his tongue against hers, dipping it between those cherry-ripe lips. Something about that small, needy action tipped him over the edge of his own grip on control. He speared his hands into her hair, silky smooth against his palm, a sensual slide against his skin as he cupped the back of her head. He angled her mouth so that he could plunder and persuade, drawing small moans from her. The pins holding up her hair, already mussed from their travels, came undone, and her hair tumbled down her back over his hand at the small of her back.

In a primal move he couldn't have stopped himself from doing even if he wanted, he wrapped his fist in the locks as though binding himself to her and groaned into her mouth. He wanted to do more, take what she was offering, lay her bare to his eyes, his hands and lips, and stake a claim on each part of her. Watch her eyes turn hazy as he surged inside her, as he spilled his seed in her body.

"More." The demand punched from him and she smiled against his lips, suddenly all siren.

She took over the kiss, nibbling at his lower lip before making her way along his jaw in a series of kisses both sexy as hell but so sweet, the dichotomy only turning him on more.

He was happy to let her lead. For the moment. And damned if that wasn't a decision that had his dick throbbing in time to the elevated rate of his heart. Because what she did with her lips against his... It was as though each brush drew his soul closer to the surface, reaching for hers, sensation spiraling outward and driving the tension through his muscles until he buzzed with it.

Small, soft hands swiftly undid the buttons of his shirt, slipping inside to smooth over his chest. Nothing tentative or hesitant about her touch. All woman. A siren in his arms.

"Fuck," he growled, and took the control back.

Owning the kiss, driving into her and demanding a response from her that she seemed only too willing to give, he trailed a questing finger down her neck, hooking it in the collar of her blouse to slip it and the strap of her bra off one shoulder, baring her skin to him. He followed with his mouth and she tipped her head back and to the side, giving him access.

Like an animal, he bit into the sexy curve of her shoulder, overwhelmed with the need to...what? Mark her? Only shifters did that shit.

He jerked his head up, staring first at the mark he'd left puckering her skin, then dragged his gaze to hers, watching her through fevered eyes, obsessed with every nuance of her flushed cheeks and parted lips, the way she pressed her body in to him. A wildness wound about her. As though she'd ceded all that precious control to him.

Damned if that didn't fill him with the need to protect that favor, offer pleasure in exchange for power, truly giving her the control. Take care of her every fucking need.

Gods she was gorgeous. "Delilah," he murmured.

The name fit her in this moment. Historically, Delilah had been a temptress, and she was every inch that, breasts thrust out, back arched, the musky scent of sex blending with her light floral scent.

Her dark eyes widened on a gasp. A flash of vulnerability lit her gaze before her expression shuttered, long-lashed lids hiding her from him.

No. The primitive imperative inside him eddied and shifted, the need to possess and at the same time share, expanding within him, making his chest tight. He didn't want a quick fuck with this woman, a tussle in the sheets to sate mutual need. He wanted...

Damned if he knew what.

"Don't do that. Don't hide." He released his grip on her hair to smooth his hand down her back, pressing her body in to his, thrusting his hips in to her so she couldn't mistake the hard ridge of his pulsing erection.

"I—" Her tongue peeked out, moistening lips already glistening and swollen from his kisses.

Then she stepped back. The way she let go of him in a deliberate, jerking motion, both hands held up, hit him like a bad spell.

Delilah shook her head, her long hair rippling out behind her, her body still all fire while her expression turned icy. "You don't know everything about me, Alasdair. You'll—"

"Still want you." He stepped in to her again, cupping the back of her neck, willing her to stop shutting him out. "I'll still want you, dammit."

The words tripped over themselves to get out of his mouth, even as shock rippled through him at the impact. When had lust for a woman he'd set to keep tabs on—and only that—turned into a need that seemed tied to more than just gorging himself on her? Into something...deeper?

Blackness consumed his vision before either of them could react to the stark admission.

Only this time, somewhere in the darkness, Delilah disappeared from his arms, like smoke in the wind.

"No!" he yelled, panic giving him a good kick.

Her floral scent lingered even as he reached out in the black, futilely searching for her. Before he could call her name, light returned. Alasdair sat perfectly still, temporarily disoriented, taking in his surroundings. More than familiar, he had to ask himself if he was in the past or now in the present.

Alasdair sat in the circular room where the Covens Syndicate met weekly. Situated on the western slopes of the Sierra Nevada mountains in California, the modern behemoth the covens had chosen to erect fit the image he projected himself. Slick. In control. But with hidden corners and edges. Constructed from cement, steel, and glass, the structure was a marvel of modern-day architecture. Meant to intimidate all. Not just the witches and warlocks they governed, but anyone who might think about coming at them. Plenty to fear in this world.

He didn't have to turn to know the waiting view outside the windows at his back was incredible. This room sat over the tops of the trees and craggy mountaintops to the towering peak of Half Dome in Yosemite in the distance. He sat at a long metal and glass table facing the doorway. Where he always sat. Surrounded by the other members of the Syndicate. Powerful mages all, including his own sister, Hestia. A group of witches and warlocks of various ages, their faces all cast in blank judgment, which was nothing new.

Where's Delilah?

A brisk knock at the mahogany doors sounded. "Enter," he called. Or the memory of him called.

This felt like it had in that alleyway when he'd witnessed the entire scene from inside himself. Observing, remembering, and experiencing all at the same time.

Delilah strode in, dressed to send his libido into overdrive, appearing her usual elegant self, her dark hair coiled at her nape, loose tendrils framing her face, lust-inducing figure set off beautifully in black slacks and a cream-colored cashmere sweater that he itched to push down over her shoulders. Only now that he knew what lurked beneath that icy control, all he could see was her fire. The taste of her skin, a new memory, layered over the old memory, and damned if his initial reaction that day—one of unwanted, ill-timed desire—didn't ratchet up a whole other level.

Like the way getting closer to a lightning strike increased

the intensity of every sense. The sound louder, flash brighter, the sizzle of pure energy tingled along his skin.

Behind her entered a woman with dark red hair. Greyson Master's now new bonded wife, Rowan. This was her trial before that marriage, when they found out who she was.

"Ms. McAuliffe?" Alasdair's previous self said. Deliberately he injected a bored sort of uncaring in his voice. Nothing covered fierce emotion better than boredom.

Rowan nodded, and he shifted his gaze to the woman at her side. Dark eyes, a twinkle of amusement sparking at him, like she'd known what he was doing a second before, met his gaze dead-on. He had to resist the need to sit up straighter. Holding onto that air of ennui, he lifted an eyebrow. "And you must be Ms…?"

The woman gave him a cool smile which, contrarily, only made his cock ache worse. "Delilah," she said in a throaty voice that didn't help his current situation in the slightest.

Mother goddess. If he hadn't met her in that moment in time…if things had gone differently…different choices…he would never have gone to her today with the demon problem. He wouldn't be stuck in this recycle of his life with her. And he wouldn't know she tasted of cherries.

"First or last?" the old version of himself asked.

Delilah said nothing, merely held her polite smile and his stare. Rare to find someone who didn't back down under his gaze. Even one as polite as this.

After a long, intense moment, he let it go, turning back to Rowan. "I'm Alasdair Blakesley, current head of the Syndicate. Greyson has filled us in on the situation and"—he flicked a glance at Delilah—"supplied us information provided by various witnesses."

In a disorienting flash, Alasdair found himself outside the memory looking in, Delilah materializing beside him as they watched their previous selves together. The voices in the room continued to go through the scene, but, body still thrumming with pent-up sexual tension from both the kiss they'd shared and the memory of their first meeting and his own realization—fuck, no wonder he'd wanted her so badly, so immediately.

The woman from that alley had starred in his fantasies for years. Had some part of himself recognized her? Or was it recognition of his reflection, of someone just like him in the ways that counted most?

"Screw whatever I'm supposed to be learning from this," he muttered.

Pure, frustrating-as-fuck yearning had him turning his back on the room to step in to her, backing her up until she hit the wall, even as her chin came up—defiance and curiosity staring at him, a heady combination when it came from her. He pressed his body against her.

He lowered his head, hovering where he could watch her eyes. "You know what I wanted to do to you that day we met?"

Her walls were still up even as he could feel her heart fluttering against him. "Kick me out of the building?" she quipped.

His lips tipped up in amusement. "No. I wanted to do this."

With slow, deliberate moves he undid the top buttons of her shirt, never taking his gaze from her eyes as he parted the fabric, pulling both sides back to expose her shoulders, then farther down. She remained still, lips parted, and didn't protest when he traced the lacy demi-cups of her nude-colored bra. Her nipples poked through the material, as though reaching for him. He glanced at her expression, waiting for her to say no. She didn't, so he dragged the cups down, releasing her breasts to his eyes, rosy tips peaked, begging for his mouth.

Her gaze flicked over his shoulder to the people—the

previous versions of themselves and the syndicate—still talking in the room.

"Don't look at them. They don't matter anymore. Look at me," he commanded.

She gave in to him, a small victory but still one he'd relish as she focused in on him intently, silently daring him to take what he'd wanted to take that day and every day since.

Watching her expression, he rolled one of her nipples between his fingers, her whimper lodging in his chest before traveling south in pulses.

"If you're going to say no, goddess," he said. "Do it now—"

She shook her head, hair still down, framing her face in tousled waves. "I want this," she whispered in that sexy, husky voice of hers, her body restless against his, pressing. No more ice or wariness in her eyes. Only heat, unadulterated, unhidden, all for him.

Thank the powers. This was how he wanted Delilah. Completely undone. Wild. For him.

"Good." He pressed into her softness, claiming those luscious lips again. Plucking at her nipple and swallowing her moans. Gods, her taste—soft and decadent and yet with a bite—could become addicting. Better than bourbon. As heady as magic. Like energy and aching and pleasure all in one.

She tugged at his lower lip with her teeth, then sucked, demanding more, and his cock surged.

A change in lighting flashed—dark than light, but slower than a blink—and he lifted his head, both of them panting. They'd moved locations again. He knew exactly where. The hallway inside the Syndicate building. Not a soul in sight.

Their second encounter that day. Who gave a shit? He was more interested in *this* encounter.

Roughly, Alasdair yanked her skirt up, trailing a hand

up her quivering thigh, then brushing it over her panty-cover mound. Soaked. For him. Already.

"Hell," he groaned, thrusting his tongue into her mouth, imitating what he had every intention of doing with his cock.

Her hands found their way to his pants, which she undid, pushing both those and his boxer briefs down until he sprang out, turgid and pulsing, into her hand. She squeezed, hard, milking his cock with a viselike grip, and his hips bucked against his will.

If he let her keep that up, he'd come faster than he ever had as a callow youth. "Slower," he begged.

"Like this?"

Drawing back, they watched each other as she pumped her hand down his length in long, endless strokes. In retaliation, he played with her over those wet panties, brushing at the bundle of nerves hidden underneath until she was thrusting into his touch.

Inching back the elastic edge, he slid a finger into her, her inner walls gripping him, slick and soft. In a second, he'd replace that finger with his cock, but right now, he couldn't look away from the play of emotions over her expressive face.

How could I ever have thought her cold?

Lust reflected back at him, the same haze of need that held him captive, but more was there. Trust. The glitter of excitement. And a wariness that wrapped around his heart like barbed wire, cutting deep. Compelling him to make this so fucking good for her, she'd never look at him like that again.

"Delilah."

That was his voice. Turning his head, he found the ghosts of both of them standing in the hallway.

Delilah's previous self turned to face him. "Yes?" she asked.

Only now, instead of frost in her eyes, he caught the

flash of something else. Something hotter. There, then gone, hidden away. Holy shit. How had he missed that last time?

The woman in his arms stirred restlessly, and he pumped his finger in her, deliberately adding the push of his thumb against her clit, grinning like a fool at the audible hitch in her breathing. "Don't look away," he said.

"Your manipulations worked out," the memory of himself said.

She raised her eyebrows coolly and said nothing.

"That is the only reason I'm allowing you to walk out of here unchallenged and unscathed."

Her head came up in challenge, and damned if, like that day, his gut response was a combination of respect and a deeper throb of need.

"I'll keep that in mind," she said.

She turned to go, only to be stopped by his hand on her arm, his touch insistent. He remembered suddenly how he hadn't wanted her to go. Not because he was angry or irritated or threatened, even though he was, but because of her. He'd been...fascinated.

And resentful of that fact.

"I don't make this warning lightly," he murmured. He'd needed something to say.

"I believe you."

"Stay away from my people."

Now she cocked her head. "I'll stay away from them if they stay away from me and my clients."

There. That moment was when he'd decided to keep a close eye on Delilah. Personally. A decision that had led him...here.

Previous Alasdair's lips thinned.

"You didn't like that," Delilah in his arms said, rolling her hips in time to his fingers, which he kept pressing in and out of her.

"I was pissed at myself because I admired your response, and—"

Previous him kept talking. "I understand you have quite a varied clientele. That could prove…difficult."

She shrugged, attitude plain. His problem. Not hers.

He considered her in silence, and she refused to look away from his stare. After a moment, his lips hitched in a shadow of a smile. "Will you at least contact me if witches are involved?"

Delilah pursed her lips and he could remember thinking only of how he wanted to suck on her lower lip until she melted. "I can't make guarantees," she said, "because it may depend on my client and the privacy privileges they hold with me. But I will when I can. That's the best I can do."

He inclined his head, though his jaw hardened. "Fair enough."

She glanced down at his hand still on her arm. She hadn't flinched at the burn mark down one side of his, seeming more interested than repulsed. "May I go?"

Alasdair turned his head to meet the eyes of the real woman in his arms now and stopped the movement of his hand. "That was the moment I decided."

"Decided what?" she asked, bucking against him, chasing a touch he refused.

"To get you into my bed. One way or another." Like that day, he smiled. A real one that had her own eyes widening in response, and she sucked in a sharp breath.

"I'll see you again, I'm sure," the old him said. And both of them walked away, leaving the current versions alone again.

"That's all you wanted? A quick fuck?" she demanded.

"What I wanted then and what I want now are… different." Hell, how could he admit that what he'd wanted then was more than a quick fuck, but he'd only realized that today?

This time, the understanding sent a chill of trepidation down his spine. Not enough to stop what they were doing, though.

Delilah tossed her head. "Actually…a quick fuck is all I have to offer. Right now. Before the real world intrudes. Take it or leave it."

She was going to say more. He sensed it. Knew it for a certainty, somehow. But she didn't, clamping her lips shut.

A quick fuck was in no way, shape, or form good enough. He wasn't stupid enough to say so, though. "I'll take what you can give me. For now."

And he'd bind her body to him through sheer need. No way was one time going to be enough, for either of them. He'd figure out how to reach the rest of her when this was all over.

They stared at each other for long, unbreakable moments. A battle of wills. Of needs.

Then she moved against him restively. "I guess you better fuck me, then," she said.

Alasdair shook his head and crooked a finger inside her, absorbing the way her body shuddered with that small movement. "Ask me, Delilah. Tell me what you want."

The battle raging in those dark eyes might look like fury, but her quivering, hot little body told him to wait. To give her this. She needed to surrender and at the same time, give him permission. The ultimate form of control.

Desire lit in her eyes, turning them almost liquid as her lips tipped in a challenging smile. "I want you to make me come so hard I see the edges of heaven."

• • •

I can't believe I said that.

The shock still didn't stop her from bucking against his

touch, chasing the high he promised to give her.

He's going to hate me when he learns what I am. I shouldn't be doing this to him.

It likely hadn't been obvious to Alasdair who or what had been binding her powers that day as a child, or what kind of oath she'd been speaking, but he was going to figure it out sooner or later.

Which meant this might be her only chance with him.

Emotions and needs twisted up in each other until Delilah hardly knew which way was up. The part of her that had been in charge—of everything—for so long...that part needed this. Needed him. Needed to let go and let someone else take the helm. Especially when he could make her feel like this.

Shockwaves reverberated through her as the import of that hit.

Ever since she'd been old enough to truly understand what happened that day her father made her bind her powers, she vowed to never let anyone make a decision for her ever again.

This is different, though. Just sex.

But even that small voice in her head knew better. Knew this wasn't just sex, though she had no idea what it was.

Today's events were like a speed round of life. Experienced together, making the moments all the more real, shared and accepted. The way she'd started the day on opposite sides from this man...those lines had blurred.

She hardly had the chance to flash through all of that before her mind blanked out as Alasdair leaned down and pulled a swollen nipple into his mouth, sucking. Hard.

A zap shot straight from that erotic draw to the junction of her thighs where his fingers played. She whimpered and felt his smile against her skin just before he did it again. And again. Rhythmically. Until her entire body convulsed to the tune of his mouth. Then he moved to the other breast, and a rush soaked her panties with the first flick of his tongue. Her entire world narrowed to his mouth, his hair, thick and soft against her fingers, as she held him to her, and the pounding swell of sensation taking over her body.

Suddenly he tipped his head back, gaze skating over what she knew had to be her flushed features, the way she'd dropped back against the wall, breasts thrust out to him, lips parted. An answering flush graced his skin, his pulse thudding hard at the base of his throat, muscles straining the fine linen of his shirt as his strong hands grasped her by the hips, blue eyes darkening, so intent on her. Reaching out to her. Like the first time she'd seen the ocean—powerful, incredible, and hypnotic.

"Gods you're beautiful," she murmured, reaching out to trace the angles of his face ending at the small indent in his chin.

His eyes widened slightly, followed by a smile this side of feral. Pure possession glittering at her.

"I need to taste you." A demand. Rough-voiced. Pulling at her almost as effectively as his mouth on her breast or the crash of those ocean waves. The sound a manifestation of his touch—rough, hard, and yet infinitely gentle.

Where had the part of her that despised demands disappeared? Because she was already eagerly nodding, her hair tumbling forward over her breasts, dark against her skin, teasing her sensitive nipples, the contrast of the soft strands after his insistent mouth and plucking tugs of his fingers sending ripples through her.

Rather than helping her out of her skirt for easy access, Alasdair slowed things down. He eased the material higher, already hitched up from earlier, drawing teasing patterns across her skin with his fingers, his lips. Kisses that reminded her of soft, warm rain and lazy days in the sun, even as each touch drugged her senses, even as she wanted…more. Finally—oh gods finally—he gently peeled her panties down her legs, helping her step out.

Then, still gentle, yet somehow more urgent, he spread her legs wider, until he had her positioned exactly how he wanted her. Only to return to the torturous, teasing caresses that built her need while at the same time not fulfilling it.

She dropped her head back against the wall, eyes closed, reveling in every sensation he was drawing from her body and not thinking about what waited for them outside this memory. What he'd do when he discovered why she couldn't help him. Every nuance, every sense, was trained completely and utterly on him and what he was doing to her body.

The man was a tease in the best way.

Hovering over the throbbing heart of her, he paused.

"Look at me," he said, his voice practically a growl now.

Delilah obeyed without giving it a second thought, as though compelled in a way no person, let alone a man, had ever engendered.

He knelt at her feet, head tilted back, staring at her. Spearing her with that gaze again. Commanding. Utterly in charge, and yet, an edge to that expression told her he wasn't entirely in control.

She'd done that to him. And she hadn't even started touching him back yet. Anticipation trembled through her.

"Don't look away," he directed. "I want you to watch me make you come."

Her breathing hitched at the mere thought that sensual picture created. "I won't look away," she said.

And power surged through her as his breath punched from his lungs in a whoosh. He liked that. Liked her submissive.

Her lips curled in a smile as she thought about what she'd do to him when he was done with her. Wicked, wonderful things. Only, what she had in mind needed them to be out of this dream world, where she could use her powers.

His gaze zeroed in on her lips, curiosity sparking in the blue. With a wicked smile of his own, he slid a finger inside her, then out, then two, filling and yet not enough. Slowly, in and out, her hips moving in time as he watched her and she watched him.

You wanted him from the moment he lifted that stupid eyebrow at you. But she'd been able to resist when she'd thought of him as a power-hungry asshole.

When she was back to whimpering, he added his tongue, hot and penetrating, pressing against the bundle of nerves so perfectly hard.

Delilah sucked in sharply, eyes fluttering closed.

"Eyes on me," he stopped to demand.

As soon as she looked, he was back. Everything, every sensation he'd layered until this point coalesced as he worked her with his mouth, coming together, building inside her until that touch on her clit turned into a match striking a trail of gunpowder leading to a powder keg, and everything inside her condensed before exploding outward.

He didn't let up, working her through every convulsion of pleasure gripping her body until she sagged against him, sated in a way she couldn't ever remember being. He caught her in his lap, easing them both against the wall, which didn't feel like anything, but still propped them up.

Why were they still here anyway?

Blue eyes met her gaze and, suddenly serious, he cupped the back of her head, fingers slipping through her hair against her scalp, as though holding her so she couldn't deny what he'd just made her feel. She had no plan to deny him. No thought beyond wishing the moment could last a little longer.

"My turn to taste you," she murmured. Where had that throaty, sexy voice come from? So unlike her, and yet so her at the same time. At least in this moment.

Alasdair's eyes glittered with an anticipation she could almost feel gathering in his muscles. He opened his mouth to speak but paused, an emotion skittering across his face that she wasn't sure of. Not hesitation exactly. Almost... determination.

Which was, of course, when her world went black.

Chapter Six

"Fuck," Alasdair muttered into Delilah's hair, pulling her closer as they waited to land.

Damnable timing.

"I'm really getting sick of this blinding business and not knowing where we're going next," he grumbled.

Especially when he was still hard as a fucking rock.

Grumbling was not a thing for him. Not to others at least. Not even in his head, usually. Grumbling was a sign of weakness, and a leader couldn't show any of that.

And yet, here he was…grumbling.

Her chuckle tickled against his skin and expanded inside his chest like a balloon filling with helium. For the first time in his life he was tempted to tighten his arms around her, when cuddling was the last thing he did with women.

He didn't want a quick fuck in dreamworld. He wanted more. Only what could more possibly look like? This was Delilah. He still had no idea what powers she held. Hell, she'd refused to help him with this demon problem beyond embroiling him in this Dickensian misadventure. As the leader of the Covens Syndicate, he knew it was expected that he would find a partner from among his own kind. A partner as dedicated to his people as he.

That word—partner—pinged around in his head like a pinball, lighting up different spots in his mind in rapid succession.

Before he could even begin to unravel his thoughts, hampered by his pulsing dick demanding release and short-circuiting his brain, the darkness lifted. They were back in her office.

Swinging out of his arms, Delilah quickly rearranged her clothing, though her panties hadn't come with them and her hair had to stay down because the pins were on the floor somewhere else. Mental note, whatever wasn't attached to them apparently didn't move with them from place to place.

Alasdair allowed himself a small second to admire the rumpled, sexy version of this woman. He'd done that. He'd unraveled her.

He wanted to do it again, but he had bigger responsibilities. Bigger needs. He needed to stop letting this alternate universe distract him from that.

He glanced around, wondering what vision was next. Another trip to her past, probably. Except…the scene was too familiar, as though they'd just left it. The papers were still scattered on the floor from when Hazah had sent him back.

Maybe they were in the present now?

The landscape outside the windows showed night had fallen. The Denver city lights had cast a pink glow across the sky, mountains no longer in view, Christmas lights strung up all across the tops of buildings in an array of twinkling colors, stars doing their best to compete with the ambient light.

Night already?

That reality jerked him out of the fantasy he'd allowed himself to stray into.

Dammit. They'd been in Hazah's lessons too long. His people—

"Something's wrong," Delilah said, urgency in her voice.

"Wrong?" he asked. "How?"

"This isn't—" She shook her head. "This doesn't feel the same. Like it's not part of the visions, or it's warped somehow. Can't you feel it?"

Alasdair focused his senses outward, frowning. She was right. The air felt...damp, heavy here in a way it hadn't anywhere else in the memories they'd been sent to witness.

"You certainly took your sweet time." An odd voice sounded from the darkness, similar to the dark rumble of a dragon shifter. By the windows, the shadows twitched. Then twitched again until the darkness seemed to writhe as a form appeared and solidified.

A man, or something the shape of a man, stepped into the soft glow of the lamp on the corner of Delilah's desk.

Demon.

Not one inhabiting a human body. It was beautiful in a way most humans couldn't stand to be around, driven to heights of jealousy by features both bold and perfectly balanced. The ultimate physical specimen. Except for the pitch-black eyes.

"This is not good," Delilah whispered as she inched closer to him. A rare display of apprehension?

"How?"

"I think he's actually here with us," she whispered.

"Are you sure?" he asked.

The demon suddenly smiled, razor-sharp teeth on display. "*Are* you sure?" it asked.

Fuck. Visions weren't supposed to respond to them, were they? Maybe they were doing that "in body" thing again?

Black eyes glinted in the lamplight. "I must thank Semhazah for this," the demon murmured. Almost conversationally. "It took a little work, but trapping *you* without the ability to fight me was just the opportunity I've been looking for."

It looked at him as it said the last.

Alasdair flung his arms wide, palms spread, willing his power to manifest, ready to hurl a lightning bolt at the thing. Only...nothing came.

Not a spark or a fizz. Impotence wasn't a feeling he'd ever had to deal with before this disaster of a day. Not even the night he'd had to kill his father.

The demon's smile echoed the seven hells, terrifying and fascinating at the same time.

All the thing needed to do was touch one of them and it could seize their body...but also control their gifts, once released to the real world. Exactly why anyone with magical powers kept up wards to prevent possession. But without his magic, he was vulnerable.

So was Delilah.

The gut-level instinct to protect had him stepping in front of her, shielding her with his body. Almost as though that move pulled the trigger on a gun, the demon surged across the room. Powerful as fuck and coming right at him. Alasdair braced himself one second, only to have Delilah shove him hard the next. Not expecting the attack from behind, he stumbled to the side and she jumped between him and the demon.

"No!" he shouted, reaching out. A useless gesture.

The fear—not for himself, but for her—that slammed through him came with a labyrinth of rage and shock that this thing dared to threaten her. That he could do nothing to stop it. Nothing to protect her in this moment. That he might have to kill her, too, if it took hold of her.

The demon clamped a hand around her arm and Alasdair expected screaming, or sizzling, or for the thing to turn into black smoke and enter her body through her nostrils. Or something. He'd never witnessed a possession as it happened. Not even his father's.

But, like with his powers a second ago, nothing happened.

The demon frowned, adjusted its grip, confusion rippling across its features. "What are you?" it hissed at Delilah.

"I—"

Its eyes grew wider, and somehow, impossibly blacker. "I know you. You're the woman who killed my windigo."

"Let go of her, Belial," a female voice sounded from behind it.

Hazah was here? She knew this demon?

Her colorful caftan flowed out behind her as though wind whipped around her despite being indoors. She stared down the creature still latched onto Delilah, who stood eerily still, never removing her gaze from the thing. Hazah, meanwhile, seemed to morph before his eyes. No longer the siren of a woman he'd met earlier today. This was a warrior—fierce, deadly, and pissed. Anger crackled in the air around her.

Heels and all, Delilah took the demon by surprise with a cartwheeling maneuver that both broke the demon's grip on her and hurtled her to the other side of the room near where Alasdair stood.

The demon sneered but kept its focus on Hazah. "You have nothing to do with this, Semhazah. You already have a body, and I have orders."

Orders? Body?

Hazah's eyes shifted subtly, turning inky black, just like the demon. Just like Agnes's demon eyes in his office.

A demon?

"No fucking way." The words burst from him.

Delilah, when he'd asked for help with a demon problem, had sent him *to* a demon. A fucking *demon*. One who'd locked them in this powerless state.

"You will have to go through me," Hazah said with a

bloodthirsty smile that sent a chill down his spine.

"Kill you and finally fulfill my task, all at the same time?" The demon—named Belial, apparently—set his feet wider, getting ready to charge. "Must be my lucky night."

Before the thing could attack, a man manifested in the center of the room, landing in perfect superhero pose, massive white wings outstretched, armor so gleamingly blinding, he hurt to look at.

Alasdair gaped at the spectacle. The man may as well have dropped down from heaven.

"Delilah," Hazah snapped. "Touch the mage."

In a blink, Delilah reached out and placed her palm over Alasdair's heart, that spot on his skin warming instantly, almost painfully, at her touch.

Blackness consumed his vision. The last thing he heard in that room was Hazah snarling at Belial. "You won't touch my daughter—"

Silence. Darkness. Shock.

"I'm sure you have questions," Delilah said. Quietly. Calmly. Way too calm for what just happened.

Fuck it all, he needed to see her face, but the void was blanking her out. Alasdair grasped the first emotion that bubbled to the top of the cauldron inside him. "Hazah is your mother?"

"Yes." Her voice was a glacier of ice in the darkness.

"A gods damned *demon* is your mother?" He was snarling now, but that couldn't be helped.

Bile stung as it rose up his gullet, leaving a sour taste on his tongue. A demon had forced him to kill his own father. The same evil was taking over his people, wreaking havoc and only getting worse. He should *hate* what she was, but... Hell, he'd just taken her to paradise, and wanted to go back there with her. What did that make him?

A blind idiot led by his dick. That's what.

"And your father?" he asked, words clipped. "Also a demon?"

Did demons have wings? Was that why the result for her cat had been death? Because she was a spawn of the hells?

"No. That would be the angel who landed beside my mother," she answered, the words stiff as though she couldn't quite make her lips work.

He had to stop himself from physically pitching forward to try to get more air into his lungs as those words sent reverberations through his entire system. Alasdair covered his eyes with his hands, pressing hard with his palms, waiting for the aftershocks to stop thundering through him.

Half demon was bad enough, but half angel, too? That was way worse.

. . .

No. No. No. No…

The word was blending together in her head, turning into useless, nonsensical sounds, feeling as though Zeus himself were hurling thunderbolts after her, one after another.

Watching the horror in Alasdair's eyes before they'd plunged into darkness tore at her like a son of a bitch. More than just about any other experience she could bring to mind. Which meant she was way further down the road with him than she'd intended to go.

She needed to focus.

A demon—Belial, her mother had called it—had somehow hijacked them. Pulled them half in and half out of her mother's spell, or maybe stepped inside it himself, so that they remained vulnerable to attack.

Razors of fear slid around her heart, slicing deep, threatening to bleed her out like an animal to slaughter. That had not been a lower-level demon—that had been a sentinel—

not once an angel, like her mother, but the most powerful of the demons who'd originated as human souls. And Alasdair's forehead had glowed with its mark in her office, which meant that thing was the same one who'd been after him since he was a boy.

Which meant Alasdair had to be integral to whatever the demons were planning. If that was true, then he needed to be anywhere but here.

They landed without warning, and the soft light had her blinking after the darkness. Delilah frowned as she looked around. Why were they back here?

They stood once more in the circular meeting room for the Syndicate. Only this time night had fallen, the snowcapped mountains hardly visible outside the blackened windows and glare of the lights on the glass.

Alasdair's chair was the only one in the room that remained empty.

Those in the room were dressed up in various levels of festive clothing. For their own Christmas Eve celebrations? Was this the present? The group didn't seem to be doing much, or perhaps they were waiting. They almost acted unconcerned, if anything. Chatting to one another softly, casually.

"What is this?" Alasdair asked.

Delilah reached for her powers, but nothing came. They were still in the visions. "I think we're waiting for whatever happens next."

But in the past or present?

"In that case..." A gasp escaped her as Alasdair grabbed her by the arm, though his grip remained surprisingly gentle, given the urgency in every line of his shoulders, and swung her around to face him. "I'm sure we don't have long, but I need answers. Explain. Now."

She stared into hard eyes of the same man who, only

minutes ago by way of normal time, had just had his mouth on her body, gifting her with pleasure beyond pleasure. He glowered at her, expression mostly closed, only she'd swear confusion lingered in his gaze.

Don't give up on me yet, she silently begged him.

She cleared her throat. "My parents' affair was forbidden. Angels and demons are sworn enemies, opposite sides of the biggest political issue in existence."

The man before her said nothing, just waited.

"Demons were once angels. According to human belief, Lucifer apparently became so impressed with his own beauty, intelligence, power, and position that he began to desire for himself the honor and glory that belonged to God alone. The sin that corrupted Lucifer was self-generated pride."

"I've heard the story. Are you saying human history got it wrong?"

She shrugged. "According to my mother, Lucifer disagreed with God about humanity. In humans, he saw such capacity for evil—for selfishness, entitlement, pride, and violence—that he didn't understand how God could want to forgive them over and over. Bless them. Meanwhile, angels, also his creation, were nothing but tools to serve God's pets. Not creatures deserving of blessings or forgiveness in their own right."

"What does this have to do with you or what you are?" A muscle in his jaw ticked. "Please tell me Lucifer isn't your father."

"No. And as for why I'm telling you…you'll see why this is important."

He paused, searching her gaze, then waved her to continue, though she could tell he was at the end of his tether.

"Lucifer *chose* to fall to escape. He wanted nothing to do with humanity anymore. Other angels followed him for various reasons of their own. Demons—true demons, who were once angels—aren't evil, necessarily. They're just... apart."

Alasdair crossed his arms. "You can't tell me that *thing* that took over my father wasn't evil. Or the one that just attacked us."

"Am *I* evil?" She tossed the words between them. And held her breath, because his answer, right this second, was... important.

Beyond a slight flexing in his arms, he chose not to respond, and disappointment tunneled a pit in her gut.

She took a breath and kept going. "To punish Lucifer, God sends all the damned human souls to join him in hell, most for punishment, but some becoming lower-level demons themselves. Not as powerful. Lucifer and the other angels who fell with him decided to turn those souls against humanity. *That's* what we've encountered so far."

"That thing we just left behind was a lower-level demon?"

She shook her head. "Belial is a sentinel. The most powerful of the lower-level demons. They must want you badly."

His jaw tightened at that. "And your mother? What's her story?"

"She was once an angel. Semhazah was the leader of the Watchers, a group of angels who spent much time on earth among humans, sometimes observing, sometimes interacting. She made the mistake of agreeing with Lucifer about human nature and fell with him, leaving my father—her greatest love—behind. She doesn't agree with Lucifer's plan, his use of evil souls, and so she...left. Left Lucifer. Left the hells. She lives apart. Still away from my father, but whenever he was assigned to earth, he would visit her."

She knew her smile reflected the sadness inside her because Alasdair shifted as though uncomfortable.

"Eventually, I was conceived."

"Fuck me," Alasdair muttered.

But did he believe her?

"As punishment after my birth, my mother was returned to the deepest of the hells. It took her many millennia to claw her way out again, and yet, he waited. All that time. So did I. Having me was the worst thing that could have happened to them. I'm…" She tilted her head, trying to hide her feelings now. "An abomination."

Anger sparked in his eyes, and Alasdair opened his mouth. "Don't you ever—"

But a man entered the room through the wide double doors that had been closed, and Alasdair cut himself off to watch closely.

"Micah, where is my brother?" a younger woman seated at the table demanded. One Delilah recognized from the first time she'd met this group of people in this very room. Hestia. Alasdair's sister. "We cannot wait any longer. Have Rowan come in, please."

Micah stood where Delilah and Rowan had stood the day Delilah had met Alasdair. Tall and with the posture of a fighter, the man's expression darkened ominously. "I don't know."

"Fuck," Alasdair grumbled beside her as Micah left the room. "This is now. The present. I ordered Micah to convene the Syndicate. But that was hours ago. Why have they waited this long to act?"

"Rowan, maybe?" Delilah murmured beside him. "You told whoever you called to bring her in."

The witch had been raised by a demon. If anyone knew anything about how to deal with this problem, she might.

The doors opened again and two people entered. Greyson Masters, Alasdair's head witch-hunter, and Rowan Masters, his new bonded wife.

Rowan stopped so abruptly inside the room that her red

hair tumbled into her face. "Grey," she said, an urgency to her voice.

He whipped his head to stare at her, searching her face.

"It's worse than I thought," she said. Her voice trembled. Then she glanced at Micah and gasped. "Grey...get us out of here."

In an instant, her husband took Rowan's hand and the two teleported away. Papers flew and the doors slammed shut in the wake of the whirlwind the spell caused.

"Oh gods," Delilah gasped.

Rowan would recognize possession when she saw it. If she ran rather than stayed to fight, it had to be next-level catastrophic.

"*No*." The word ripped from Alasdair, and she flinched at the sound. She'd done this to him. Sending him to her mother. He could have been here to stop it.

Almost as though they'd heard the word "demon," every person in the room slowly turned their heads, eyes filling until the orbs were glassy soulless black. Those gazes pinned Delilah where she stood. Evil intent pierced her with their looks.

Whispers filled her head and Delilah clamped her hands over her ears against them. *"It's her,"* they said. *"The child. The abomination. Kill her."*

"Delilah?" She was vaguely aware of Alasdair calling her name, of his gaze swiveling between her and the demons who'd possessed every single one of the Syndicate members. Except him.

As one, the demons rose to their feet. Coming for her.

"Mother!" Delilah cried out and threw her arms around Alasdair's waist.

Darkness.

"Goddess help us..." Alasdair whispered into the void, his body ramrod straight against her. "The Syndicate has fallen."

Chapter Seven

Delilah landed back in her office a blink later. Immediately, Alasdair stepped away from her. Jerked away, actually, and, precariously balanced on her stiletto heels as she'd been, Delilah fell right onto her ass. He grimaced and held out a hand, helping her to her feet, though even that small touch communicated his emotional state, the tension vibrating through her like a tuning fork.

He dropped her hand and started toward the door. "We have to go."

"Wait," she said. "I don't think this is over."

"Dammit," he snapped, not at her but the situation.

Honestly, she was on the same page.

Delilah glanced around. The room looked like a tornado had torn through it. Windows busted out. Glass everywhere. Furniture and papers everywhere. Bookshelves toppled. Her laptop, or at least the top half of it, somehow lodged in the drywall.

"Mom?" she called out.

Nothing.

"Mom? Dad?" Delilah called again, trying to breathe through a well of panic. They'd been together. *Together.*

"Delilah."

She and Alasdair both spun around to find Naiobe standing in the doorway, a paleness underlying her mahogany skin that gave her an ashen hue.

Delilah rushed to her friend, checking her over as she did. "Are you okay?"

"I'm unharmed." Naiobe laid a hand over Delilah's, stopping her inspection.

"Don't lie to me," Delilah said softly. "It makes your nose twitch."

Naiobe sighed. "Just a small scratch, easily healed." She held up an arm with a welt that looked close to a week old.

Thank the heavens for small mercies.

"The demon?"

"Gone. Your parents sent it back to hell."

"Holy shit." The words burst from her before she could stop them. It must have been worse than even she'd imagined.

"Your father is safe. Your mother is unharmed as well." Naiobe grimaced. "Or at least, she will be able to heal from the wounds she sustained."

It had been *that* bad? The fact that thing had managed to wound her powerful mother said a lot.

"In here," Naiobe said.

Her friend pressed her palm against a hidden spot on the wall. A scanner beeped and turned green, then a click and a large section of dragonsteel disguised to appear like wood paneling swung open, revealing a hidden panic room—supernaturally warded, of course.

Inside, her mother lay on the floor, her back propped against the steel wall. Delilah's father, no longer in armor, instead in jeans and a white cable-knit sweater of all things, knelt at her side, his blond hair a disheveled mess, which spoke volumes.

They were still together? Goddess above.

Delilah hurried over and dropped to her knees on her mother's other side. Her father reached out to squeeze her arm, and Hazah cupped her face with her hand. "I'm all right."

But Delilah could only shake her head. "You're both here," she whispered. If she hadn't sent Alasdair to her mother...

"Why is that bad?" Alasdair asked from where he stood in the open doorway.

The question sent her muscles into spasming tension all the way up her back. Holding herself stiffly, composing her features, she angled her face toward him.

Were this any other man, she wouldn't bother to explain. But this was Alasdair, and she'd surrendered too much to him to hold back now. Besides, deep down she *wanted* him to know the truth. Though no doubt it would do little to alter his opinions. The way he stepped back as soon as they'd arrived... The man could hardly stand to be near her.

"They are forbidden to see each other."

"Because of you." A statement rather than a question.

"Watch it," her father, usually so reticent, growled.

Except Delilah blinked, her gaze on Alasdair's face. She knew this man in full sarcastic dick mode. That hadn't been accusation. More like...acceptance. Didn't he hate her? Hate what she was?

He tipped his head, ignoring her angel father and demon mother to look directly back at her. What was he saying with that silent, steady stare?

Delilah glanced away, at Naiobe, to cover the confusion racing through her heart. "Get yourself somewhere safe."

Her assistant, and one of the three people who knew everything about her, part of the deal for Delilah releasing her from her bottle, hesitated. "But—"

"Promise me," Delilah insisted.

The Syndicate had fallen, Alasdair was marked, her parents were together and injured.

And Delilah could do nothing.

Nothing but push Alasdair away before she made things worse.

. . .

Alasdair felt as though he were being ripped into a thousand pieces as loyalties and needs pulled him in too many different directions.

Still reeling from every damn revelation over the last what had felt like fifteen minutes at most, his heart slammed against his ribs like a wild animal trying to break free of a cage. The panic room seemed to close in on him, too quiet for his mind, which was still processing everything.

Dammit.

Alasdair stared at Delilah, a dull ache taking up residence in his chest, gripping his insides with fists made of stone. Not because he hated her, but because she thought he would. He could see it in the confusion swirling in her dark eyes.

But this day had changed everything. He could never hate her.

Because she'd turned out to be that woman in the alley. Because she'd been trying to help him, even if things had only gotten worse. Because she'd wanted to give the child version of him a hug. Because she'd tasted like heaven coming all over him.

She was part demon…and he didn't care.

He should. She'd lied by omission. That relevant fact could've been shared at any time in their dealings today. Hell, the second he'd told her he had a demon problem, even more so after she'd witnessed the scene of his father's death.

That vision.

Mother goddess, was that what he now had to face? How was he supposed to stop the demons if they possessed the most powerful witches and warlocks in existence? His sister among them. Was he destined to lose his entire family? The damage the Syndicate could do, must already be doing…

"Why does Belial want me?" he asked.

"You're the leader of all mages and extremely powerful." Hazah's voice sounded like sandpaper had been taken to her larynx. "They have seen your future as part of their plan, whatever it may be."

I need to go. Now.

But he was trapped here, in this *Christmas Carol* catastrophe, while the world was falling apart, and Delilah's pale face and the way she wouldn't look at him was making his heart wrench.

He held out his hand. "Come with me."

Her eyes went wide, and she gave her head the slightest shake. "I can't—"

He jerked his gaze to her mother. "Release us from the visions," he demanded.

"Watch how you address her," Delilah's father said. Quietly, but no doubt that was an order.

Alasdair didn't have time to ask nicely. "The Syndicate has already fallen. I have to save my people."

The demoness closed her eyes, then frowned, shaking her head. "I am too weak to see if the future has changed. I can't see…anything." She opened her eyes. "But I won't hold you now. The legions are coming."

Legions? Icy claws of fear raked through him. "Why?"

Hazah's smile took visible effort. "If you were trapped in hell and possession was your only way to get out and stay out, you'd do it. You'd do anything, try anything, kill anything you had to after long enough. But demons' attempts to break their eternal bonds have been thwarted too many times by powerful creatures up here. Taking over mages not only to keep those people from sending them back, but to use those powers for their own purposes is…brilliant."

She was right. If he'd been trapped down there, he *would* do anything to get out. With that kind of motivation against him, *could* he even stop this?

"I hope what you've seen is enough to get you through." Hazah waved her hand.

A flash of darkness, like power flickering off and on, and, immediately, a sharp pain, like a hot poker jammed into his skin and melting through to the bone, flashed across his chest. With a hiss, he yanked back his shirt to find that spider mark from Hazah gone.

His *Christmas Carol* was over. They were done. He had no doubt. But they weren't nearly finished with what was to come.

He lifted his gaze, offering his hand again to the woman still sitting in a heap on the floor beside her mother, and froze halfway there at the sight of her expression, gone so blank, so uncaring, she might as well have punched him in the face.

"Delilah?"

She rose to her feet slowly, chin tipped up at that haughty angle that used to make him so damn frustrated. Still did. Anger stirred in his breast, swirling with a hurt betrayal that was worse by far. After all this…was she going to let him face this alone?

He could see the truth of it in her eyes before she spoke.

"I can't go," she said.

"Why?" he snapped the word.

She shook her head. Was she refusing to tell him? "Just go. You can't—"

Her mother cut her off. "When my daughter was born,

both factions—angels and demons—feared the power a child of both could hold over them. Neither angels nor demons can affect our daughter. But with the blood of both in her veins, she could destroy an entire species if she wished. At least, that was the concern."

Dread dropped over him like a blanket woven of lead. He turned his gaze on Delilah. "*Was* the concern?"

She glanced away, then back, then shook her head.

"The binding won't let her speak of it," her father said quietly.

Alasdair looked over her shoulder to find a man tormented by the actions he'd taken against his own daughter.

Every horror of that decision written plainly in the lines of his face, the deep regret in his eyes. "That spell that bound her powers was an unbreakable oath. She can't help or harm either side. Anything to do with angels or demons and she must stay out of it."

Alasdair dropped his gaze to Delilah's face, finding... nothing. She watched him carefully. Held herself carefully. And he had no fucking clue what to say to this. "Or what?" he asked.

She shrugged, still distant. "I've never tested the limits of the consequences."

Why was she acting like this? Every duty, every fear, the weight of his people and possibly the world, rested on what happened next, and he found that he wanted...needed...her at his side. What were consequences in the face of annihilation? "Come with me anyway. Do what you can."

Delilah stilled like a doe in the forest with a hunter's bow trained on her heart. And, for half a second, he thought she was going to reach for his hand. But then she drew herself to her full height, hands fisted at her sides. "No."

The single hard word, uttered in cool control she'd perfected, dropped between them, seeming to *thud* on the ground like a dead body dropped from a great height.

After a long beat full of disbelief and betrayal, Alasdair shook his head. She couldn't mean it. The woman he'd come to know today, hell the woman he'd learned of this past year and in that alley, wouldn't walk away from someone facing supernatural peril.

"I don't believe you," he said, slowly. Softly. "What aren't you telling me?"

She tipped up her chin. "It doesn't matter if you believe me. I'm *not* coming with you, and you're out of time."

She glanced at her father, who, after a pause, waved a hand, and without a will of his own, Alasdair was sent away.

Chapter Eight

He hates me.

His expression as he disappeared told her that much. She'd made him hate her so that he could go. So that he *would* go.

The series of emotions that had crossed his face when he'd learned of her binding had moved too fast for her to catch every nuance. She'd expected the worst. Accusations. Incriminations. Instead, what she'd seen was the one she'd secretly, selfishly been hoping for.

Understanding.

Even though he no doubt blamed her for the entire fiasco of a day, he'd understood and wanted her with him anyway.

I would push the limits and risk any pain, for you. The words had hovered on her lips, feathering through her soul as though sewn into the fabric of her very makeup. But she'd held back.

He'd given her an orgasm. He'd fought beside her against the windigo. He'd comforted her in the worst moment of her life.

That was it. So small in the scheme of things, and yet cataclysmic to her personally.

Every part of her had focused on not giving away how that understanding, from Alasdair in particular, with his own history, made her want…things.

Things he couldn't give her.

Not with his past—his father's possession and what that had made Alasdair do as a child—and the blood in her veins. Worse, was something she knew that he did not. What always ended up being the point of the visits to the past, present, and future.

The future visions always—*always*—showed how trying to ignore or test her binding was the worst possible thing Delilah could do.

After her mother clawed her way out of the hells and discovered her daughter's powers constricted, Hazah had used these lessons to instill blinding fear into Delilah about the consequences. That unbreakable oath—to neither harm nor help either side with her powers—had bound her with magical shackles for the rest of her immortal life.

She'd found ways around her limitation. Helping others who needed her. As long as her actions had nothing to do with angels or demons, she was fine. No bone-deep agony and no potentially world obliterating outcomes. That's what every other future vision her mother had sent her to had shown previously.

As much as her heart wanted Alasdair, her mind knew that whatever he felt for her, as chained as she was, she was worthless to him. If anything, she would be in the way.

She'd only make things worse.

I made the right choice, sending him away. For the first time in her life, she lifted her gaze to heaven and prayed.

Prayed that he survived. That he triumphed. Because God help them all if he failed.

Her mother suddenly made a small sound. A whimper. A noise Delilah never in a thousand millennia thought she would hear her strong fighter of a parent make.

"What?" Delilah and her father demanded at the same time.

"What's coming," her mother said, voice turning more thready with each syllable uttered. "It's worse…"

Her mother could see the future? Wasn't she too weak? If she went any paler, Hazah would pass out.

Her father clutched her mother's hand, anguish crossing his features. "Semie? Don't do this. You don't have the strength."

"Do what?" Delilah demanded, glancing between them. What was happening?

They both looked at her. Why did she suddenly feel like the little girl she'd once been, looking for approval from both her parents and never quite finding it. Their natures were too opposite to allow for that, even if they both loved her more than anything, and still loved each other. In their own way.

"I have to—" Her mother waved her hand.

The darkness of yet another vision dropped over Delilah like the harbinger of doom.

• • •

Even in the void of nothing, before landing at her destination, the pulse of magic sent the pressure around her climbing, pushing down on Delilah, making her ears feel like they might pop and bleed any second, just to relieve it.

Then the darkness lifted and she stood at the edge of a massive crater, debris from what, at a guess, used to be the Syndicate's headquarters littered the ground in chunks of white cement and twisted metal, the stench of ozone all around, and dust clogging the air. Alasdair's people lay dead or dying in the rubble. White sparks of…whatever had blown the structure to kingdom come…continued to ignite, like a glittering pantheon of fist-sized fireflies that would flare to life and burn out in a blink.

Incongruously, snow lightly fell over the scene, pristine and clean, like some horrible cosmic joke.

She closed her eyes against the sight. How far into the future was this? Was Alasdair too late? Had he already failed?

I'm sorry.

She wanted to go after him now. Warn him before this happened. Before it was too late. Only she was trapped here, in a future that would come to pass if she didn't figure out how to change it.

The future. Always the crux of her mother's lessons.

So pay attention, she told herself.

A boom echoed off the mountain peaks in the darkness, followed by a red flashing glow and several screams. Another boom, and something dark whisked past her in the darkness, sending a spiderweb of shivers over her skin.

Demon.

A huge blast from the direction of the crater practically shook the mountain under her feet and her vision blacked again only to come back so fast, she would've wondered if she'd blinked if she wasn't looking at a different scene. Still in the wooded mountains surrounding the area where the Syndicate's headquarters had once stood, she stared at the bald side of a mountain.

This area was worse than the last.

Bodies littered the boulders and ledges of the mountain, strewn about like tissue paper after a child's birthday party, limp and lifeless. Only, as she watched, darkness appeared to leak from each like liquid smoke dripping out of every orifice and pooling on the ground before reshaping and reforming.

Another hundred demons at least.

"Merciful heavens," she whispered.

Horror clawed at her insides like a trapped feral cat, and she could do nothing. Impotent in this scene. Unable to help even if she were not in a vision. Damn her oath.

With another flash, she appeared in the bottom of the crater. Whatever had blown this had to have been massive because she stood at least a hundred feet below the top. As though the explosion not only took out the structure but disintegrated the giant flat-topped mountain of pure granite the structure had been built upon. The area was glittering. Not from the firefly-like sparks, which still popped up all over the place. Now, the sky was lit by a strand of lightning stretched overhead, but frozen there, blinding to look at directly, casting a blueish flickering glow over everything.

Just enough to see Alasdair—the future Alasdair—facing off against a legion of demons, some inhabiting bodies of witches and warlocks. His people. Some still in shadow form. Black eyes flashed at him in the spitting, hissing light of the electric bolt she had no doubt he'd put in the sky.

"Teleport," she whispered. Urging him with her entire being to get out of there. Forget horror—*fear* clawed her raw from the inside out. "Get out of there."

She was practically rocking as she willed him to listen, despite knowing he couldn't hear or see her.

But he didn't leave. Of course he didn't. This was Alasdair.

Something—she wasn't sure what—caught his attention and he lifted his gaze up, way up. She turned her head, following his eyeline. Over the lip of the crater, a pair of red glowing eyes appeared, seeming to hover in the blackness, beyond the reach of the lightning bolt. Only after staring hard did a faint outline make itself clearer.

Hellhound.

Then another set of eyes, and another.

Three hellhounds.

Seven hells. These demons weren't fucking around. Even her mother knew better than to mess with those dogs. Unpredictable and able to kill with one bite, injecting poison into their victim that slowly ate them from the inside out.

Suddenly, one shadow broke from the others and sprinted toward him so fast it blurred with the speed. Without a word, Alasdair reached into the sky and formed a glowing energy orb, purple and brilliant. The demon backpedaled but not fast enough. Hurling the orb, Alasdair smashed it into the shadow, which disintegrated on the spot.

Then another came at him, smashed the same way. And another, and another, until the hoard overwhelmed him, and he went down under a pile of shadow demons, his face a mask of determination even as he disappeared from her view.

Everything inside her body cried out, convulsed with emotions she hadn't allowed herself to access in ages. For Alasdair.

Delilah took jerking steps forward, desperate to dig him out from under, an impotent fury joining the fear. These fuckers—no matter if she carried their blood in her veins— dared to touch him.

A glow penetrated through the nooks and crannies of the pile of bodies and then burst outward, an explosion that sent every demon flying, leaving Alasdair standing by himself. Not for long, as they regrouped and came back at him. With a whispered spell, he drew more electricity from his body, stretching it out into a whip. Grasping one end, he flicked it at one, then another. Then he spun it so fast, it blurred, like the propeller of a plane. Turning in place, he took out every shadow demon that came at him.

Why weren't they using the hellhounds or the demon-possessed bodies yet?

Almost as soon as she had the thought, all three massive black dogs charged down the embankment of the crater with deep, scratchy howls that put the fear of the hells into her.

"Alasdair!" she screamed. Not that his future self could hear her.

Even so, he jerked his head up, tracked the hounds, and then muttered another spell. His body lifted into the air, wind whipping around his form as he gained the pinnacle. He lifted a hand and a bolt of electricity shot from the sky to his body, as though he were a lightning rod. Then he dropped to the ground and punched that charged fist into the rock.

A blinding flash of light followed immediately by a sizzling boom, and even Delilah's ears in her protected vision reacted with ringing. After several shakes of her head, her vision and hearing cleared only to find the shadow demons and all three hellhounds now piles of ash at Alasdair's feet.

A shout of challenge rose up from the possessed, a rumble of sound, like a storm over the ocean. In a wall of movement, they rushed him. Only, he didn't use the lightning now. Not against his people. Kill the demon, kill the human it inhabited. She knew that he'd learned that the hard way with his father.

Choices and consequences. Stepping-stones to this moment. Even without witnessing the aftermath again today, a lesson he wasn't likely to ever forget.

At first, spell after spell tumbled from his lips, clearly doing his best to take them out with other means. Some dropped to the ground in a deep sleep, some flew away or disappeared, some froze in place as though bound by an invisible force.

But mages got their power from within, and he had to be running low by now, risking his life to continue using magic.

Each spell affected fewer and fewer until the numbers swelled over him like a tidal wave and he went under. She waited. Waited for him to get out from under it like he had only moments ago. For him to fry the demons. But he didn't. He wasn't coming back up.

Delilah, heedless of how this was only a vision, sprinted toward him. Before she reached him, though, the bodies suddenly flew away, as though one of the gods had reached down from the heavens with his great fist, scooped them up, and tossed them away.

Thank the gods—

The thought stopped stone-cold inside her mind as she caught sight of him. Delilah tripped and fell to her knees. Heedless of the rocky ground, she gaped at the man now standing at the center of the demon horde. Pitch-black eyes in a chiseled face now as familiar to her and dear to her as her own.

Alasdair. But not.

He'd been possessed. The red glowing mark on his forehead, turning brighter by the second, told her what had him in its thrall. That same fucker who'd been after him all along. The world was fucked.

She had enough time to suck in an audible, painful gasp before her vision went black.

Chapter Nine

Delilah's father had sent him to the forested mountains of northern California, just outside the Syndicate headquarters.

She'd made him leave. Had him sent away.

Delilah.

Everything inside him screamed and strained to go back and get her, but he couldn't. He curled his hands into fists at his sides, pushing the devastation of losing her—because that's what had just happened—down into the dark recesses of his soul.

She was right. He was out of time.

With a whisper of a spell, he teleported to the building. Alasdair didn't use the landing pad officially created for teleporting use, a spell that tended to be windy on takeoff and landing. The wards around the Covens Syndicate building prevented arriving or departing within the walls as a precaution against magical invasion.

His wards. Ones he'd put in place himself.

Which meant he could break his own rules. So he bypassed the pad to appear directly in the main chamber where the members of the Syndicate met. The *possessed* members, now. The windows rattled a protest at his sudden, slightly violent appearance.

"Dammit, Alasdair." This from Abernathy Khan, the oldest of their order. "Rules."

Fuck, the demon inside his old mentor was good. That was exactly what the real Abernathy would have said.

Don't believe it. It's not him.

He ignored the old man, looking around. Two empty chairs now. His and… "Where is Hestia?"

"Behind you, big brother."

Alasdair tried not to stiffen, calling on that control that he'd lost sight of today as he'd gone through all those visions with Delilah. Because that might be Hestia's voice, but his sister never called him big brother. Ever.

"Good. We're going to need you," he said, pretending to be ignorant of the demon inside her.

Inside his sweet younger sister, who'd been raised separately from him because she cried every time she saw him and had to remember what he'd done to their father. Who he'd hardly known until they were both adults, when he'd discovered that she cried because she hated what he'd had to witness and go through, not because she blamed him. Anger seeped into his bones like poison, and he had to physically hold back his own power. He was going to need it for what was about to come.

He had to stop this. Here and now.

A *whoosh* of sound, soft as hummingbird wings, was the only warning he had before Delilah suddenly appeared in the room next to him. Right in front of him, back to the others so she could look up into his face, hers deadly serious, paler than her usual shade of cream. She glanced around and he could have sworn relief flitted across her expression.

Relief?

"I just saw the future," she said, dark eyes intent.

And came rushing to him after so adamantly refusing to come with him? Not only that, she was relieved to see him in a room full of demon-possessed mages? Whatever she'd seen must've been horrific.

"Let me help," she said. "Please."

Begging? He couldn't allow that from this amazing, tough, brave woman. He reached for her, but a voice stopped him.

"Alasdair?" Hestia circled around to face him. "Why is this...person...here?"

He ignored the facsimile of his sister, focused on the woman in front of him.

Delilah didn't move by so much as a twitch. "Trust me," she mouthed.

• • •

Even the thought of what she was about to do had the bindings around her wrists clamping down so hard, keeping the agony from her face was a battle of sheer will. If Alasdair knew, he'd send her away.

The instant she'd landed back in her office, the significance of those sparking lights around the crater in that future vision had struck. *This* moment, right now, would start the entire battle. Because Alasdair was going to blow up the building. He had made that crater in the future.

Not even her mother could have predicted that, or Delilah had no doubt that vision would have started in this room instead.

The man stared down at her and she could see the battle in his eyes. Who'd already betrayed him by refusing to help once? Would he trust a woman whose blood was half demon? She wasn't remotely confident that she'd make a difference.

Her vision hadn't gone beyond what happened *without* her here. After seeing that...no fucking way was she letting him face this alone.

Alasdair's expression settled, determination there in the cold set of his jaw, and utter, incredible trust in the blue of his eyes. "Okay, goddess. Call the shots."

She couldn't let the burst of relief at his words distract her. He wasn't going to like the shot she called. Neither was she.

Wrists already screaming in agony, she turned slowly.

Pain leaked from her eyes in rivulets down her cheeks that she ignored even as her skin now might as well have been dipped in dragon fire. She put out a hand, palm facing them, feeling the essence of each demon in the room. Lower-level demons. Her mother had once explained that escaping the bounds of the seven hells was easier when the signature you put out, due to a lower power level, wasn't as easily traceable.

Exactly what Delilah had been hoping for.

These were placeholders for the more powerful demons to come. Which meant, thanks to her mother's stronger demon blood—the original blood of angels—in Delilah's veins, she held sway over these foot soldiers.

With a grip on the demons' essences, she dropped two words into the silent room of watching demons and magi. "*Idimmu Alka.*"

Demon Come.

Then formed a fist and jerked it toward her.

As the demons screamed a protest at being forcibly wrenched from the bodies they inhabited, pain lit up every single nerve ending in her body, radiating up her arms and down her spine and outward. Agony sent her to her knees.

"Delilah?" Alasdair's voice barely registered.

"When they're out," she managed to choke. "Take the others and go."

"I'm not leaving you—"

"*Please.*" She wasn't beneath begging. Not for his life. "Trust me."

Even if she died in the process.

The last demon, shadow seeming to hold on to the body it had claimed by the tips of its claws, finally slipped free. "Go!" she shouted.

In an instant, wind battering her, he was gone, along with every other human in the room.

"Impossible," one of the shadows hissed.

Delilah didn't stop, though.

Summoning the strength to push through the pain, she spoke again. "*Ati Me Peta Babka. Alik.*"

Gatekeeper, open your gate to me. Go.

A whirlpool opened at her feet, sinking into the polished marble flooring and leading to the seven hells. A cry rose from the shadowy forms as, one by one, they were sucked inside, sent back to the first level of hell where the gatekeepers would determine what to do with them. Their own terror spiked through her heart, shards of ice joining the blistering heat consuming her.

This one act made her a traitor to her own kind. These were half her people, only wanting to escape the hells in which they'd been trapped. No more perfectly evil than the angels were perfectly pure.

Her parents had taught her that.

But she had no choice. If the demons found their way out in numbers, they would consume the world. Alasdair and his people were *not* going to be their gateway. Not if she could help it.

Only, the whirlpool started to drag at her own body.

Oh gods. She'd forgotten to protect herself with her summoning words. The hells wouldn't differentiate between demons' souls.

Scrambling, she tried to teleport herself away, but, as though vines had wrapped around her ankles, she felt herself being pulled inexorably into the void.

She tried one series of words, then another, the slick floor giving her fingernails no purchase and her spells doing nothing. As though the words and her power were consumed by the portal she'd created.

As she was dragged in, black spots appeared in her vision, slowly narrowing to a pinprick. Then something grabbed her by the wrists and a scream tore from her mouth at the instant, bone-shuddering agony. But whatever it was didn't let go, pulling at her so hard, she thought her spine might snap from the strain of the opposing forces.

"Don't you give up on me, dammit."

Alasdair's voice.

No. He shouldn't be here. He needed to be out there with his people. Fighting. Because more demons were waiting. She knew that for certain from her trip to the future.

"Let me go," she begged.

"No fucking way."

But she slipped in his grasp, sweat—his, hers—making her skin slick.

"Dammit," he muttered.

Then two more sets of hands landed on her, one on each arm and, in a massive tug, she was freed of the whirlpool, landing in a heap, half on Alasdair, by the scent of his cologne, and half on the cold stone floor. But the whirlpool was still going. It wanted all the demons in the room.

A familiar voice—her father's voice—uttered an incantation, and the sound stopped along with the drag on her body. Delilah slumped forward, catching her breath, aware of the rise and fall of Alasdair's chest. She shook her head, clearing her vision, and lifted her head, that small action shaking her whole body, to find both her parents kneeling beside them.

"Mom?" she choked through a throat constricting around too much emotion. "Dad?"

They weren't supposed to be here. Her mother was too weak, and it went against every rule on both sides.

Hazah cupped a hand to her cheek. "You will always be my baby."

Her father took her by the hands and helped her to her feet, then whispered words that sent a cooling rush over flaming nerves and healing the oozing blisters and boils that had formed around the circumference of her wrists. Not removing her shackles, but soothing her so that she could keep going. He yanked her into his arms, and for the first time ever, showed her an emotion, his body shaking against her.

"We've tipped our hand," he murmured in her hair. "If we do anything else to help—"

Their own people would come for them. "I know."

She took a deep breath, stepping back to look at them both, maybe truly seeing their love for the first time. "I love you."

Before they could respond, she gripped Alasdair's arm and whisked just the two of them to where instinct told her his people were gathering.

They appeared on the mountainside, at the top looking out and over a small, snow-covered valley. One filled with hundreds...no thousands...of mages. Not possessed yet, she didn't think. Here to fight. Their chanting filled the night air with the heavy weight of powerful magic.

A glance to her right showed her Rowan and Greyson Masters both there. Had they left the Syndicate in order to bring others? Thank the gods, because they needed all the help they could get. Rowan, her mouth moving with the words of the spell, nodded her head in acknowledgment.

In the same moment, Alasdair whirled around, taking her by the shoulders. "Dammit, Delilah. You've done everything you can. Clear out of here."

She shook her head. Whatever happened next, she couldn't let the future she'd seen come to pass. There would be nothing left for her if it did. "No. We do this together."

Already, the healing her father had wrought was replaced by a clamping heat. Air hissed through her nose as she sucked in.

Alasdair opened his mouth and then jerked, eyes going wide. Darkness bubbled up from the ground beneath his feet. Smoky shadows rising up—a legion of demons swarming their way from the pits of hell. Several mages tried to defend themselves, spells lighting up the darkness in bursts of color, and flame, and ice, and more. But it happened too fast. The shadows found bodies and filled them up.

Alasdair included.

In front of her, darkness took over the man she'd sworn to fight beside tonight, seeping in through his nose and eyes and mouth. So fast. Too fast.

His gaze darted to her, face contorting grotesquely. "Run," he mouthed. Then his eyes rolled back in his head, the sockets turning inky black, and the sigil on his forehead started to glow.

No. Gods no.

This wasn't how it was supposed to happen. A quick glance around showed every witch and warlock in sight going through the same transition. The same possession. Leaving her utterly alone.

Despair slammed through her like a spear to the heart. But she didn't have time. No way could she extract every demon with the same spell she'd just used. Only one option entered her mind.

"I'm not running, Alasdair Blakesley. I love you too

much."

Burying her fear in the deepest recess of herself, she whispered a word, manifesting a dagger formed of light and energy in her hand, then grabbed Alasdair's wrist and slit open his veins before doing the same to herself, only to have to bend to the side and vomit at the pain. But she held onto him and, as soon as she took a breath, mashed their wounds together, mingling their blood, binding her soul to his. Magic as ancient as creation itself. Nothing would separate them after this.

If he died, she died. If he fell, she fell.

It was also a desperate attempt to fill him with demon blood, making him impervious to the creature trying to take over his body. The shadow sort of stopped moving, as though someone had hit a pause button, as though it had hit a wall inside him.

Please. Please. Please.

The horrible agony around her wrists disappeared suddenly, the angry red welts dissolving. As though Alasdair's blood and magic had done the inconceivable, had broken her binding. Was it even possible?

Relief punched through her. It had to be working. It had to be.

She watched Alasdair's face closely as the pulse of blood flooded between them in rapid, surging spurts. Black eyes, pits of unfathomable darkness, stared into hers. And then he—or the demon inside him—smiled and the glowing run on his skin pulsed, like a taunt. The man before her wasn't Alasdair...he was Belial in possession of Alasdair's body. She could see the damn sentinel in the darkness of those eyes.

"Now part of *you* is human," Belial said in a terrifying version of Alasdair's voice.

More smoke rose from the ground. It swirled, creeping up her skin, and a chill overtook her sending a shiver wracking through her as a different demon entered Delilah's own body. Almost like everything she was had been shoved to the back of a pitch-black ice cave, so cold it burned.

I can't let them take either of us. She and Alasdair were both too powerful to be captured and used by demons.

With the last of her conscious will, pushing from that blackness to control her limbs, Delilah lifted her dagger to her throat. After all, if she died, they both died.

• • •

Was this how his father had felt the night Alasdair had had to kill him? As though his very soul was being buried deep. In the darkest, coldest recesses of himself. Except he could still hear and see what was going on, what was happening. Watch as the dark smoke of a demon infiltrated Delilah's body. Watch the despair wash over her features. The terrible decision she made as she raised the sharp blade to her throat.

"No!" he shouted, the word echoing inside him, bouncing off the walls of his insides.

In that moment, everything about his life, about the past that Hazah's spell had shown him, coalesced. Before, he could see only the individual threads, but now he had a broader view and could see the entire tapestry. Delilah didn't need to tell him. She'd come tonight because the future that her mother showed her was worse. That meant worse without her here.

He'd assumed that also meant Delilah was the key to victory. After all, she'd sent all those demons possessing the Syndicate members back to hell, giving his people a fighting chance.

But that wasn't what the visions had been showing them. Alone, they'd had no choice in the most important events in their lives. But the fates had brought them together, thanks to

Rowan. The windigo. They'd defeated it—

"Together." His whisper swirled around him, casting out the chill invading him.

Before he could do anything, though, he had to wrest back control of his body. Battle for his very soul.

Belial—even in here he recognized the demon—felt as though his insides were coated in tar, sticky and scorching.

Rather than struggling to push the creature out, Alasdair drew on his power and yanked at the other being invading his insides and pulled it down deep to where he waited. He closed his eyes as he whispered a spell, and pictured the one place he knew better than any other in the world, the place where he had grown up secure in the loving bosom of his family before demons had ripped them apart.

Their family home by the lake.

He infused his magic into every nook and cranny of the vision so that when he opened his eyes, he stood at one end of the family room, a soft glow of a yule log in the fireplace penetrating the darkness outside the window. The sounds, the smells, the feel of the rooms so real, he almost believed it himself.

At the other end of the room stood Belial in his demon form, the fucker who'd been trying to possess him his entire life.

This is my house, asshole.

The demon glanced around as though shocked to find himself somewhere new. Then his gaze landed on Alasdair and his expression hardened, promising black retribution.

There were only two ways out of this hell of being trapped in his own mind while this demon took possession. Force it out or die. Alasdair had no intention of dying. "Foolish of you to try to take me," Alasdair taunted.

"More are on their way," the demon hissed. "Strike me down, and another shall take my place."

Alasdair's magic crackled, electric sizzles skating over his skin, standing his hair on end as he gathered more and more inside himself. The demon's own power oozed through the room, filling the space with the scent of sulfur, making it difficult to breathe.

Without warning, instead of reaching for his most potent ability of electricity, Alasdair spoke the words that would awaken the wards in the house. Wards his father hadn't had a chance to engage the night he'd died.

Instantly, the cement floor rose up like fists and wrapped around Belial's feet. At the same time, the tongues of flame from the fireplace reached out and wrapped around the demon's wrists. But Belial laughed and then disappeared, becoming the black smoke that a physical world could not contain.

The smoke shot forward, coming for Alasdair, who summoned a bubble of glass around himself. The smoke bumped up against his glass container, curling back on itself. Then it coalesced and condensed and the demon solidified and manifested a club—solid black and shiny, like onyx. With one swing, Alasdair's glass protection shattered.

Needing space for what he'd do next, Alasdair hurled a bolt of lightning so strong, the boom of sound deafened him for a second. The thunderbolt struck Belial in the chest, throwing the demon backward, legs and arms flailing. It slammed into the stone wall, which seemed to reach out and wrap around him, yanking his body into the masonry of the house. This time, Belial uttered a single word—the secret word that turned off the wards in the house, something only Alasdair's family was supposed to know—and the wall released him. Spat him back out into the room, whole and sneering and smug.

Alasdair scowled, recognizing that the demon, in possession of his body, was using his own powers and knowledge against him. This was getting him nowhere. He couldn't defeat this thing. Not on his own. Not trapped inside himself like this.

Together.

Delilah was here with him, inside him, in this room with him where she'd asked just today if anyone had thought to give him a hug that horrible night. He could feel her, in his blood, in his soul.

Alasdair knew what he had to do.

A whispered spell and in his hands appeared a relic, a weapon like the rope he'd used on Agnes, that his father had hidden within this house. The very weapon he'd used to help kill his father and the demon inside him as a child. Chains with shackles at the end, ones that had once held a saint in prison. He threw the chains at the demon, another spell shooting them across the room, binding them to Belial's wrists and ankles and dragging the demon across the room to chain it to the wall.

Immediately, the demon thrashed and screamed in agony, the putrid scent of decay and rot filling the room, but that wasn't enough. The chains had killed the demon in his father, but Delilah had said Belial was a sentinel. Stronger.

Alasdair closed his eyes and reached out. Reached not for his powers, which the demon had taken equal control of, or the demon's blood now flowing through his veins. Instead, he reached for the gift her father had given…angel's blood.

Light filled his vision, and warmth seeped into every pore in his body, as Alasdair started to chant. A simple spell. The words seemed to flow into him, as though guided by an unseen force. The light pulled away from him, coalescing as a ball, floating in front of him, and the demon's eyes widened. Even in those black pits, fear was visible.

Now it was Alasdair's turn to smile.

With a whisper of a spell, he sent the light careening into

the demon's chest. Chained as it was, nothing it did could deflect the orb. The second the light touched it, the demon screamed. It didn't stop screeching as it disintegrated into the black smoke it had been. But the light didn't stop, penetrating every piece of darkness inside the mirrored room Alasdair had created, the glow blinding.

The cries of agony cut off abruptly as the last wisp of smoke was obliterated, and Alasdair pitched forward, hands on his knees, breathing hard.

He'd killed the demon. Decimated it. Belial would never come for him again.

He didn't have time to celebrate—Delilah and his people still fought for their own souls.

In a blink, he returned to himself, right in the moment Delilah had brought that blade to her throat, as though time had stood still while he battled.

She went to slice her jugular, only Alasdair grabbed her by the arm. "Not yet."

• • •

That was the *real* him speaking, and Delilah sucked in a sharp breath as his eyes cleared, turning piercingly blue, even in the dark of the night. Then tingling swept through her blood, flowing to every part of her. The demon trying to take her over syphoned out of her in a damn hurry, becoming shadow once again, writhing on the ground in swirls of contorted darkness, as though in pain.

"Hold onto me," Alasdair told her. "And say these words with me."

Without question, she clung to his solid form and listened, then started to repeat the spell he was chanting. Words of angels and demons. A spell of...light. A spell using their combined powers, but especially calling upon her father's angel blood now inside them both.

She could feel the power coming. The tingling turning to a building rush, and pressure, as though her blood was turning to crashing waves in her veins. The spell inside them both built and built until, a cry tearing up her throat, gripping him hard and locked in arms that turned to steel bands around her, they both threw their heads back and light burst from them, filling the night sky until the world turned sunlight bright.

A terrible cacophony of shrieks rose up around them, and Delilah managed to force her gaze to the side, watching in her frozen state as the light bursting from her and Alasdair passed from person to person, connecting them all in a web of purity. Every mage surrounding them froze in the same posture, backs arched, and heads tilted to the sky as illumination poured from them.

Then, as fast as the magic struck, it disappeared.

Delilah's knees crumpled out from under her, but Alasdair managed to hold onto her and keep them both upright, though his body shook so hard with the effort it rattled them both. Slowly that shaking subsided.

"What—" Her voice came out as a croak. She cleared her throat and tried again. "What just happened?"

She should be exhausted. Drained. Dead even, after that much magic poured from her. Alasdair too. But instead, her body was energized like she'd been plugged into an electric socket. Buzzing with it.

"They're...gone." His voice held a note of incredulity.

She blinked, looking around them. Not a black eye nor a whiff of smoke or shadow to be seen. Just the peaceful darkness of the night. In the distance an owl hooted, as though the forested mountains themselves were telling them all was well.

Alasdair's arms tightened around her, and she raised her

head to find him watching her with a heady combination of awe and heat in his eyes.

With a groan, he dropped his head and claimed her lips, kissing her as though tomorrow wouldn't happen, even though they both now knew it would. A whimper of need escaping her, Delilah gave herself over to the moment. The sheer bliss of kissing him back, of giving herself to him while taking her own pleasure in each frantic kiss.

"Alasdair?" a woman's voice called from nearby, vaguely insinuating itself into her consciousness. They both ignored it, too wrapped up in each other, and the relief, and the sheer, carnal need building and pulsing between them.

A throat cleared, and the woman tried again. "Alasdair." His sister, if Delilah wasn't mistaken.

He lifted his head but didn't look away, staring into Delilah's eyes as though the answers to all the questions of the universe could be found there. "Hestia, get everyone back inside. Make sure this is over. I'll be in touch…after."

After? Delilah cocked her head in question. *After what?*

Chapter Ten

Relief and triumph and a soul-stirring need threatened to pull Alasdair under, and he had only one thing on his mind. Claiming this woman once and for all.

Body on fire for her, Alasdair whispered the spell that whipped them away from his people to the footsteps of the one place he never thought he'd want to return to.

He looked down into Delilah's face as she tilted it up to him. "Here?" she asked. No fear, no wariness, not a wall keeping him out or a snowflake of ice in sight. Just trust…and an answering need that reflected his own.

"My home." He lifted a hand to trace the curves and angles of her face. "I took it back tonight."

Giving a shiver, possibly from the chill of the winter air, a soft smile bowed her lips but disappeared quickly. She stared at him with glittering eyes, lips parted, need radiating from every part of her, answering his own. "You should go back to your people."

Only the frown tugging at her delicate brows told him she hated that idea as much as he did. Even if she was right.

"I need you first," he said in a voice gone gruff.

There were a thousand and one things he should be doing. Working with his people to assure themselves all the demons had been exorcised. Determining how to prevent this from happening again. Hell, just explaining to the other members of the Syndicate what the fuck just happened would be a good place to start.

But Delilah was in his arms. Safe. His people were safe. And he was buzzing with the aftereffects of the battle, and winning against terrible odds, and her blood inside him, and the fact that she'd been willing to sacrifice herself. For him. For his people.

From deep in a dark, cold place, he'd watched in panic as she'd sliced open their wrists. But then warmth had reached him inside his mind, opening up power. Just in time to keep her from killing them both.

Even now, residual apprehension wrapped around his heart and squeezed like a constrictor. Unconsciously, he tightened his hold on her, but that only served to rub her body against his, press her against him, and blood surged south in pumping, thrumming need.

Delilah blinked at him, then raised her eyebrows, sudden mischief dancing in her eyes. Though something lingered in those soft, dark depths that gave him pause.

"You know," she said, lifting her arms to twine them around his neck, "I still haven't gotten my turn to taste you, yet."

"Thank the powers." Laying claim to those lush lips once more, he swept her up in his arms, carrying her inside. The door was never locked. Not here. His house was spelled to know him. By the time he got them to his room, they were both gasping and only halfway undressed.

Too many clothes. He needed to see all of her.

Lips not leaving hers, obsessed with that hint of cherries,

he skimmed his hands over her curves and around behind to slowly unzip her skirt, something about the rasp of that sound in his bedroom, where he'd pictured her more times than he'd wanted to admit to himself this past year, and a wave of possessive tenderness about took his knees out from under him.

He let the skirt slide down her thighs to pool at her feet, lifting his hands to cup her face so he could look at her. Drink in her beauty.

"If you'd died tonight…" Mother goddess, they might as well have buried his body in the same grave.

Delilah bit her lip, brows furrowed with a worry incongruous to the moment. Or didn't she feel this between them the way he did?

He was so far gone, he couldn't picture moving forward without her.

Somewhere along the way, he'd fallen in love with this woman, the seeds sewn well before this day finally reaching into the light, thanks to what they'd shared. Until this morning, their flagrantly different lives, his responsibilities, and her visible dislike had kept him from seeing his growing feelings for anything beyond an extraordinary physical need.

He knew better now.

She loves me. I know she loves me.

With only the idea of soothing that look from her eyes, he brushed a tender kiss across her lips, then nibbled his way along her jaw to her ear.

"I want you," he whispered, and smiled as her shiver of reaction teased his palms.

"Then we'd better do something about that," she whispered back.

Not what he'd meant exactly, but her hands were at the button of his pants, and suddenly the frantic surge of need took them both over again. With a curse, he whispered a spell that took care of the rest of their clothes.

Delilah gasped then chuckled. "Impatient?"

"Yes." He couldn't even laugh about it, the urgency gripping him so hard, tightening everything about him painfully.

A twinkle lit her eyes as she cocked her head. Then, before he knew what she was about, she dropped to her knees, fisted the base of his pulsing cock. "My turn to taste," she said, and slid her mouth down his shaft.

The sight short-circuited his brain as sensation took over his entire focus, the rest of the world drifting away as she worked his body. He speared his hands into her hair, watching in fascination as she slipped her lush lips up and down. Then she sucked hard and he came damn close to embarrassing himself.

With a grunt between pain and panic, he picked her up, swinging her into his arms. "I want to take my time," he said in a voice he hardly recognized. Amazing what this woman could do to him with just a touch. "I have a goddess in my bed. I want to enjoy every fucking second."

• • •

In the course of a single day, that nickname had turned from a minor annoyance into an ignition point, lighting her blood, which was already on fire for him.

She would have to walk away after tonight. His people would never accept what she was. Dangerous to them. A lightning rod, especially after breaking her vow. Demons would see her as a traitor. They'd keep coming.

You should tell him that with your blood mixed, your lives are linked. She ignored the voice, assuring herself that she would tell him. Tomorrow. Now was not the time.

She could have this first. Have the illusion, the dream of

tonight and a future filled with him.

Alasdair laid her across the bed so tenderly, with such reverence in his expression that she came close to crying. Tears stung her eyes. Emotions, usually held at bay, were almost overwhelming in their intensity. She took him by the hand and laid a series of kisses across the scar-pocked skin of his arm where fighting his father's demon had burned him, willing away that past pain.

With the softest of touches, his face a study of awe yet still tight with eagerness, he traced the lines of her collarbone, the outer swell of her breast, the dip of her waist. He lingered over the sensitive jut of her hip bone.

Then he followed that path with his lips, and she kept her gaze on him, trying to memorize this moment, to be brought out and lovingly examined in the small hours of the nights to come without him.

He left no part of her unexplored, lingering anytime her breathing hitched. The backs of her knees, her belly just under her navel, her shoulders, the back of her neck. Somehow, without touching the most erogenous areas of her body, he painstakingly built need inside her until every heartbeat, every rush of blood through her body, was exquisite torture.

Until she was begging for more.

Delilah wasn't passive. Exploring the planes and ridges of his body, the dusting of hair over his chest, learning that sucking on his earlobes made him shudder. That a brush of her lips over his hip bone made him fist his hands in her hair.

With arms that shook—a stark reaction he didn't try to keep from her—he rolled her so that he lay between her legs, his hot, velvet and steel shaft pressed against that bundle of nerves that throbbed harder at the pressure and the heat.

Alasdair stared down into her face, hiding nothing from her. "I need you to be mine."

For tonight. For always, she thought. But she didn't voice the words, just nodded, unable to tear her gaze away. Wanting to remember every precious second.

He whispered a spell that protected them both, one of the best parts of sex with a warlock. Then he was there at her entrance, sliding slowly, beautifully, into her body until he was balls deep, filling her.

Delilah swallowed back a cry of loss, shaken to the core at how, even with him embedded inside her, she was already missing him, her heart cracking and bleeding internally.

Alasdair ran a finger down the side of her face. "Okay?" he asked with a small frown.

Delilah nodded, hair spilling across the pillow. "Perfect."

Wonderful. Beautiful. Glorious.

He smiled and drew out of her as slowly as he'd entered her, then slid, just as unhurriedly, back home. Penetration like a claiming.

He gazed into her eyes as he controlled the pace, driving her already thundering body to a level that sent her into a hazy world where all that existed for her was the throb between her legs, the pulse of his body penetrating hers, and a pair of wicked blue eyes filled with everything she'd ever wanted to reach for.

But she couldn't let herself. For his sake.

He increased the pace and she lifted her legs, wrapping them around his waist, sending him deeper, their twin moans mingling in the night. His control snapped in that moment, blue eyes turning glitteringly bright as he surged inside her, his body shaking over hers even as she trembled beneath him until tingling gathered at the base of her spine.

Pressure pooled and collected and grew until it burst outward, sucking her into a vortex of pure bliss as violent as the whirlpool to hell that had tried to take her. And every second, she looked into Alasdair's eyes, memorizing the way his face contorted as his climax washed through him, the way his hands, fingers threaded through her own, gripped hers harder, the light in his eyes that she could almost fool herself into believing meant more.

They came down from the high together, chests heaving, sated and lethargic, the loving arms of slumber already wrapping themselves around her.

"Merry Christmas," he whispered against her lips, making her smile even as sadness slid tendrils of worry through this moment that should have been sheer contentment.

Alasdair shifted them so he lay on his back, her head on his chest, the slowing thud of his heartbeat the most beautiful sound she'd ever heard as they both drifted into oblivion. But even as she fell into that blissful sleep, Delilah knew it couldn't last.

They will come for me.

She was half demon, and they would see her choices, her actions, tonight as a direct betrayal. They would come for her and anyone near her. She could have this moment with Alasdair, but that was all.

She'd be gone by the morning.

Chapter Eleven

Alasdair walked into the outer room of Delilah's offices, dressed in his best Armani, his usual control in place, at least outwardly. He wasn't sure what her assistant, Naiobe, was exactly. Hopefully she couldn't hear the violent thunder of his heartbeat. Not even the day he'd been voted to the head of the Syndicate had he wrestled with this level of nerves and doubts.

Of course, that day, his taking the role had been a foregone conclusion, at least as far as he was concerned.

The woman who held his heart in her hands—not so much.

That fucking note.

He'd woken up from a mind-blowing night of mutual pleasure secure in the knowledge that he'd found the one and only woman he wanted at his side through life and into death to find the bed beside him cold and empty, her things gone, no trace of her beyond the scent of cherry blossoms on his sheets.

And a politely chilly note on her pillow that shredded his

heart like a cheese grater.

He'd decided to give her a week to realize what he already knew. A week. That had been an aspirational joke. Three hours were all he'd managed to wait before coming here to convince her. Of course Delilah and her assistant would be working on this holiday. He did the same himself most years. Maybe not any more, though.

This was Christmas morning, and he was going to get his Christmas miracle.

Another one. The demons had been the first.

Naiobe glanced up, her dark eyes flickering with an emotion he couldn't pinpoint the second she recognized him. If he hadn't been looking closely he would've missed the small twitch to her button nose and had to compress his lips around a grin. That had been a helpful tell to overhear Delilah comment on the other day. "I'd like to speak with Delilah."

"She's not here," Naiobe lied without even a blink of her big, deep brown eyes.

Using the serious, no-bullshit glower that got most people to move—usually with hustle—Alasdair leaned over to place his hands on her desk, leaning in to her. "We both know that's not true."

He'd timed this deliberately to find Delilah in the office. He'd also had help from two unexpected sources—though maybe not so unexpected once he'd gotten over the shock—figuring out his best move.

Naiobe pursed her lips and gave a speaking look to his hands before lifting a pointed gaze to his eyes.

He didn't move, which earned him only mulishly narrowed eyes. "She's in a meeting."

"With her parents. I'm well aware."

That finally got a real reaction, her shoulders coming back like a soldier at attention. "And how do you know that, may I ask?"

"Because they told me to be here at this time."

"I see," she said slowly, and slid a glance to Delilah's door, then back to him. Then she rose to her feet and placed her hands on her desk, mimicking his posture, going nose to nose. "You hurt her, and you answer to me."

"I understand."

She gave a perfunctory smile that did not reach her eyes. "I don't think you do. To start with, I'm a freed djinn."

Djinn possessed access to more magic than mages, not having to pull it from themselves, but from the power found in nature. Of course Delilah would have one for an assistant. She'd probably freed Naiobe herself, he had no doubts.

"You believe you understand what that means," Naiobe said, eying him. "But you don't. When I was enslaved and given that power, I was already more than human. Ever hear of an adze?"

Holy shit.

As the leader of all his kind, Alasdair made it a point to know all supernatural creatures. Adze were rare. From the depths of his memory he pulled out a general idea. "The legend in the Ghana and Togo region of Africa—fireflies who in human form become vampires?"

"Vampire is such a loose term." Her smile sent a chill through him, controlled just barely. "We like to eat fresh internal organs. Human, animal…" She gave a negligent shrug as though it didn't matter which. "I'm a particular fan of—" Her gaze dropped to his crotch.

Alasdair grinned, obviously throwing Naiobe off, based on another nose twitch. "I should have known Delilah wouldn't have just anyone as an assistant."

They stared at each other across the desk for a long moment before she gave a reluctant half smile, then sauntered to the door. "I'm not the one you need to worry about." She paused, her hands on the door handles. "I don't know what happened, but she's been... I've never seen her like this."

"She's not the only one," he confessed.

"Fix it," Naiobe ordered. Then opened the door. "Sorry for the interruption, Delilah, but Alasdair Blakesley is here and insisting on speaking with you."

He walked in to find Delilah standing beside both her parents, no shoes, and an expression caught somewhere between irritation and panic before she buried it under that layer of ice he hated.

"Remiel. Hazah." He nodded at her parents.

Delilah whipped her head around to stare at her parents. "I'd hate to think you had anything to do with this," she said through tight lips.

"Apparently, daughter, you learned nothing of the lessons I sent you through." Hazah stepped up to Delilah and placed a kiss on her forehead and whispered something he couldn't catch but that sent red flags of color into Delilah's high cheekbones.

"You have both our blessings," Remiel said, also giving her a kiss.

Then Remiel took Hazah's hand in his—a gesture Delilah's gaze shot to, and she couldn't quite disguise the vulnerability that flashed across her features—and they disappeared. No sound. No wind.

"Must be handy to teleport indoors," Alasdair murmured.

The face she turned to him was perfectly composed, not an emotion in sight behind the glacier she'd erected. "I'm sure you didn't come here to discuss my parents' form of travel."

"No."

"So, what can I do for you?" She started to move behind her desk.

"Marry me."

Delilah froze, her back to him, then slowly turned, even icier, which meant he'd gotten to her. "You know I can't. I told you in the—"

He pulled the piece of paper out of his breast pocket and held it up. "In your note?"

She glanced at it, then back to his face, and drew her shoulders into stiffly perfect posture. "After what I did to my own kind... There will be retribution, against me in particular."

Sucking in through his nose, he stepped closer to her. "The night I killed my father..."

Her eyes widened slightly, a shadow of confusion shadowing the dark depths. But she didn't stop him, so he kept going.

"I had the demon wrapped up in bands of electricity. The thing was screaming. Howling with it, and suddenly his eyes turned blue, like mine, the blackness going away, and he was my father again."

She licked her lips. "The demon pretending to be him? To trick you?"

Alasdair shook his head. "My father managed to break through, only for a moment. He said—"

The words choked off deep in his throat. He'd never told anyone this. Not even his sister. Breathe in. Breathe out.

"He said he was proud of me. That he loved me."

Delilah stepped nearer. Only a tiny bit, but that obviously unconscious gesture gave him some small hope.

"Then he told me how to kill the demon. Knowing it would take him, too."

Pain—for him?—rippled over her delicate features. Breathtaking features. Demon and angel. No wonder she was the most beautiful woman he'd ever seen.

But that wasn't what held him captive.

Her heart—he'd seen it over and over in his investigation into her, and now in their *Christmas Carol*. She took on the hard luck cases, the bleeding heart cases, the lost and pathetic, the downtrodden, the hopeless. Delilah might be half demon, but her soul was all angel.

She glanced away, breaking the connection, and when she returned her gaze to him, the frost had turned the windows of her eyes hard and cold. "Why are you telling me this?"

"Because, killing my father molded me, but differently than what every single person around me assumed. They worried I would want revenge, or turn bitter, angry. That I'd use my own powers for the wrong reasons."

"But you didn't," she said.

"Partly because of what he did that day. His reaching out to me in the way he did… I saw that love, maybe especially in death, would always be stronger. So everything I do for my people, every step I've taken, I've refused for it to be in anger or vengeance."

The corner of her mouth tilted up, even as she pursed her lips. "A good man," she murmured.

"Don't you see? That's you, too."

Her eyes widened slightly. Was she hearing him? Could she see this truth as clearly as he could?

He stepped closer, daring frostbite to reach out and frame her face with his hands. "You set up a business helping others. Whatever went into your makeup, who you are is still up to you. And only you."

She closed her eyes, shutting him out, and shook her head. "But don't *you* see? That's why I can't. The danger I'd put you in…" She swallowed and opened her eyes, all her emotions shining there for him to see. Regret. Sorrow. Pain.

Alasdair smiled softly. "Haven't you learned this lesson yet? We are always better together." They wouldn't have won this round otherwise. "And then there's the love thing."

"Love thing." She scoffed and sent him a long, cold stare. One he could see now that she was forcing. A crack in the ice she'd built around her heart. "I don't love you," she said.

A bullet to the heart would've been less painful. But he pushed through, knowing she'd just lied. "I heard you, goddess."

"You heard? Heard what?"

He nodded, grim now. Everything hung on this moment. "You said, 'I'm not running, Alasdair Blakesley. I love you too much.'" He paused, for once in his life, scared to ask the tough question. "Do you still?"

Delilah sucked in a sharp breath, then her hands shot to her cheeks. "You heard that? But...you were a *demon*!" She spun away from him. "You were possessed. You weren't...you."

Chunks were falling off the glacier now.

He finally dared to touch her, stepping closer to take her by the shoulders and turn her to face him. "Those were the most beautiful words I've ever heard."

Hands still on her cheeks, her eyes welled with tears. "No. I'll take that memory from you and you can live your life without me. Safely. It's the only—"

"Don't you fucking dare. You're the best thing in my life. Do not steal that from me. Don't disrespect me by taking the choice away. Because I would choose you every time."

Finally, the glacier thawed all the way, the sight incredible, as her face crumpled and she fell in to him, head against his chest. "Why are you making me admit this?"

He pressed a kiss to the top of her head, inhaling her subtle scent. The cherry blossoms had disappeared from his sheets after the first day away from her. "Because I'm so in love with you, not facing this and not finding an answer isn't an option."

She stilled in his arms, not even breathing.

"It would rip me apart. I couldn't stay away to give you time to think before rushing over here."

Delilah lifted her head, searching his gaze. "It's too soon," she whispered.

"I started falling in love with you long before our adventure. I just didn't admit it until your mother's ploy gave us a fast-forward button."

She shook her head. "Why?"

He couldn't contain a snort, wanting to kiss her before she came up with more reasons to keep them apart.

"For a thousand different reasons. You talk back to me, and question me, and are a general pain in my ass."

Her lips twitched. "That doesn't sound like love."

"Your entire life is about helping others who need help. You were willing to give your life for my people."

"I can still help you without—"

He put a finger to her lips. "You are my mirror. Power and position and influence hiding a core of emotions we don't show to anyone." He paused and smiled. "Except you. I show who I am to you, and I have no damn idea why. It's quite frustrating."

She went to speak, and he stopped her with a soft kiss.

"It's frustrating because you see me. The real me. Down to my soul. And thank the gods I see you, too. Every beautiful inch of you." He took a deep breath. "We are both stone-cold on our own—powerful, in control, and effective. Even with this blood binding thing, we could go our own ways and I suspect we'd be just fine. Except I don't want to be just fine with a part of myself always and forever with you. Especially if I'm right and your demon/angel blood just made me immortal."

That had been a revelatory moment.

He put his forehead to hers, closing his eyes. "Together we are nothing short of spectacular, and I don't want to miss another single second of us."

He held her tight and waited and prayed to every god and demigod and spirit and anything else he could think of. Gradually, almost as though she was letting go of her worries one at a time, the tension leaked from her body. With each small give, she leaned in to him, and he offered up thanks.

Finally, gods finally, she lifted her head, then went up on tiptoe to wind her arms around his neck and plant a soft kiss on his lips.

"I do love you, though gods know how in the seven hells that happened." She grinned, rare dimples flashing and pure delight lightening her features.

Alasdair grinned back. "And?" he prompted.

"I'll marry you. Bind myself to you any way you'll let me." The frost was completely gone from her dark eyes now, only heat and happiness reflecting at him.

"Thank heavens," he murmured, and claimed her lips in a kiss that quickly got out of hand.

Only he couldn't let it. Not until after. Forcing himself, he lifted his head, loving the flushed, tumbled, loved look of her. "Merry Christmas."

Delilah's smile was the most beautiful gift he'd ever received. "A truly merry Christmas," she murmured. "And gods bless us, everyone."

Alasdair grinned at the Dickens reference. "I'll never think of that story the same way again."

She smiled back.

"We'd better go," he said.

"Go?" She frowned. "Where?"

"Your parents are waiting with my minister of ceremonies."

Her eyes went wide. "We're doing this now?"

He cocked his head. "No way am I giving you time to rethink this." Then he held his breath.

After a long stare, she gave a delighted chuckle that shot straight through his heart before traveling to other parts of him.

"In that case," she said. "I'd better get my shoes."

Epilogue

Delilah jerked upright in bed, the sheets slipping softly down her body and her bare nipples puckering in the chill of the air.

It took her a moment to realize where she was as she came out of her own vision. But as clarity returned, she breathed in pure contentment. She was home.

A low grumble was all the warning she had before a warm arm banded her waist and pulled her back down into waiting arms, skin against skin. Alasdair tucked his head into the curve of her neck, feathering a kiss across her pulse.

"Another Seeing?" he asked in a sleep-rumpled voice.

She sighed, relaxing into him. "Yeah."

"Bad?"

"Interesting."

That caught his attention, and he blinked open, blue eyes suddenly alert. "What?"

She sighed, thinking through the images she'd just dreamed. "I'm pretty sure a cupid is about to accidentally shoot himself in the foot, giving himself amnesia, and falling for a siren at the same time."

Alasdair grinned. "Isn't a siren's job to lure foolish men to their death with her beauty?"

Delilah sighed again. "Yes. This one is going to be complicated."

That drew a chuckle from him. "My meddling wife. You just can't help yourself."

"I make people happy," she protested.

"And I love that about you." In a sudden move, Alasdair rolled her beneath him, settling between her legs, already hard and hot against her. "You definitely make *me* happy."

She rolled her eyes but couldn't hide her own blissfully happy smile. "Stupid happy." That's what his sister, Hestia, had called them the other day.

"You make me happy, too. Even if you are a control freak."

With wicked intent and a deliberate wiggle, Delilah whispered a series of words that set both their bodies buzzing with sensation.

Alasdair growled, pretending to be irritated with her upping the pace of their lovemaking, sending them almost frantic with that single spell. But his grin told her he loved it. Mostly because they were about to orgasm, over and over, for the next hour. Together.

Sometimes, it paid to have a little devil in you.

Acknowledgments

Even in the middle of a pandemic, my writing is a personal blessing. What a time to need an escape! Writing and publishing a book doesn't happen without the support and help from a host of incredible people.

To my fantastic paranormal romance readers… Thanks for going on these journeys with me, for your kindness, your support, and generally being awesome. Thank you also for your patience. I know you waited for Delilah's story for a long time. I knew the second I put her on the page that she had to have her own story—especially since I knew what she was. But then she showed up talking to Alasdair in *Bait N' Witch*, and then I had my hero. I hope you loved them!!! If you have a free sec, please think about leaving a review. Also, I love to connect with my readers, so I hope you'll drop a line and say "Howdy" on any of my social media!

To my editor, Heather Howland…my stories are always, always better because of you.

To my Entangled team…best in the business and awesome friends.

To my agent, Evan Marshall... Thank you for your constant support.

To my support team of friends, sprinting partners, beta readers, critique partners, writing buddies, reviewers, and family (you know who you are)... I know I say this every time, but I mean it... Your friendships and feedback mean the world to me.

Finally, to my husband... I love you so much. To our awesome kids, I don't know how it's possible, but I love you more every day. I can't wait to see the story of your own lives.

About the Author

Award-winning paranormal romance author Abigail Owen grew up consuming books and exploring the world through her writing. She loves to write witty, feisty heroines, sexy heroes who deserve them, and a cast of lovable characters to surround them (and maybe get their own stories). She currently resides in Austin, Texas, with her own personal hero, her husband, and their two children, who are growing up way too fast.

Discover more Amara titles…

Bane's Choice
a *Vampire Motorcycle Club* novel by Alyssa Day

Nothing is more important to Bane than protecting his Vampire Motorcycle Club from the death magic invading his territory. An ancient vampire, he seeks cold, unfeeling, bloody vengeance… until a frustratingly sexy human doctor is thrust into his path. Buttoned-up Dr. Ryan Sinclair never thought she'd find herself in a motorcycle club full of terrifying vampires. Or so intrigued by their enigmatic leader, who seems balanced on the knife's edge of killing her…or claiming her.

Pirate's Persuasion
a *Sentinels of Savannah* novel by Lisa Kessler

Immortal pirate Drake Cole has a painful secret—when the Sea Dog sank in 1795, a young stowaway, whom Drake swore a blood oath to protect, went down with the ship. The ghost of a boy lost at sea over two hundred years ago leads local medium Heather Storrey right to Drake's door. She's determined to free him from his self-imposed prison. But how can she protect him from a curse no one can see?

Arctic Bite
a *Forgotten Brotherhood* novel by N.J. Walters

Tracking Cassie Dobbs brings shifter-assassin, Alexei Medvedev, to a remote bar in small-town Alaska, where this hot-as-hell Reaper is casually serving drinks, as if she doesn't have a bounty on her head from Death himself. Alexei is dangerously intrigued. Everyone in the Brotherhood knows the first rule: don't fall for your target. They only send assassins after those who deserve to die...or so he's been made to believe. Now that he's met Cassie, though, he's not so sure.

Night's Kiss
an *Ancients* novel by Mary Hughes

Vampires killed my parents before my eyes when I was young. My revenge? I'll destroy every last one of the evil bastards, starting with their king. But only one man can help me find him. Achingly tall, dark, and too-sexy-for-his-own-good, Ryker. Now it seems evil monsters are also after our prey, and they'll stop at nothing to see us all dead. And why are we having so much trouble finding the king?

Made in United States
Troutdale, OR
06/17/2024

20622426R00092